# Waken

Melissa R. Mendelson

Cover and layout by Emily St. Marie

Copyright © 2023 Melissa R. Mendelson

All rights reserved.

ISBN: 9798389345188

# ACKNOWLEDGMENTS

Thank You Gloria, Lisa and Lee for your
love and support with my writing.
Thank You Adele for your revisions and suggestions,
which have helped improve this story.

Chapter One      1

Chapter Two      17

Chapter Three    29

Chapter Four     43

Chapter Five     71

Chapter Six      75

Last Chapter     81

## CHAPTER ONE

Shadows fell across pale, blue walls. Sunlight flickered over picture frames of family and friends and paused across the smiling faces of a beautiful couple. Time ticked softly by on the grandfather clock poised next to the wooden coffee table. Static played across the television set, and the remote lay dead on the floor. Sounds of sleep carried through the air, coming from the one beneath the covers on the couch.

A blast of music sent the sleeping figure spinning forward. A hand reached out from beneath the covers in search of the alarm clock. A quick slam of the fist, and all was right with the world. But sleep was gone. The covers fell forward, and a disheveled man wearing a white undershirt and boxers rubbed his face. Another day, another dollar, Gary thought and moved away from the couch.

Bare feet padded up the carpeted stairs, but he tried to move quietly. More pictures of family and friends met him on his way to his bedroom. The door had been left partly open, and he slipped quietly inside in order not to wake the woman lying in the bed. He opened a dresser drawer and grabbed a pair of socks, underwear, and another undershirt. He moved over to the closet and chose a black suit with a blue tie. He was all set to walk into the bathroom and prepare himself for another day, but he felt eyes on his back. She was looking at him, but he didn't want to fight with her. He ignored that penetrating gaze of hers and closed the bathroom door behind him. Fifteen minutes later, he exited the house and walked toward his car.

"Damn it," he cursed as he tried to start the ignition. "Come on!" He slammed his fist against the steering wheel. "Start. Damn it!"

He didn't want to be late, especially from waiting for a tow. He could ask her, but that would mean for them to talk. And they would talk, but he didn't want to get into that conversation so early in the morning. He withdrew his keys and stepped out of the car. He knew where all the bus stops were in town, so he would take the bus. His law office was only a few miles away, and maybe, it would take his mind off things from home.

"Morning, Mr. Javin," the bus driver greeted him after coming to a stop in front of the local convenience store. "Didn't expect to find you here."

"Morning." Gary tried to remember the bus driver. He was heavyset with a blob of brown hair, and he looked uncomfortable in his uniform. As he held the driver's gaze, he remembered something. It was a few months back, and one of the drivers of this company had raped a young woman, who had made the mistake of falling asleep on the bus. She woke up, found him inside her, and pressed charges shortly afterward. She also took the bus company to the cleaners, and with his help, they nearly went out of business. "Maybe, this was a mistake," he said, ignoring the annoyed and wandering gazes of those waiting to arrive at their destination.

"I don't hold a grudge, Mr. Javin. Sure, you got a lot of us laid off because of what happened, but you also defended my son."

"Your son?" Gary paused in his climb up the steps.

"Yeah. The cops picked him up one night walking home stoned with a bag of marijuana and a butterfly knife," the bus driver whispered as he watched Gary slowly nod in response. "He didn't do any jail time, thanks to you, and the fine wasn't as much as they said it would be. But he did community service."

"I remember, and that case was sealed." A man nearby loudly cleared his throat. "If you don't mind, I would like to take the bus today to my office."

"Anything for you, Mr. Javin. No fee." He handed back his money. "I owe you one."

"Please, call me Gary." He nodded at the bus driver and took a seat a few feet away from him.

"Some people," he heard a man say, but he ignored the comment.

Gary leaned back in his seat and turned toward the window. The Town of Waken was alive and well this morning with traffic and pedestrians. Local shops were open, and business was good, despite the big chain stores moving in. More developments were going up, and real estate was booming. Those in the seats around him were either conserving gas for their work commute or going about their daily errands, and some were like him and had no choice but to take the bus today.

He noticed a strange man to his right with a long, dirty beard and scraggly hair staring intently at him.

"Morning," the strange man spat at him.

"Morning," Gary responded and turned his attention to a pregnant girl nearby. Her hands were wrapped around her huge belly. When she smiled innocently at him, he blushed for being caught looking. She gestured for him to touch her belly, but he shook his head. He couldn't, not after what he had said to her last night. He was grateful to see his law office coming up ahead.

"Here we go, Mr. Javin. See you later?"

"We'll see." Gary stepped off the bus, and as it pulled away, he realized that the strange man was still watching him.

Javin and Henders Associates was located right on Main Street, opposite the large food chain supermarket and the strip mall that surrounded it. A large development was only a few blocks behind them. Nearby were major highways for anyone looking to cut through town or make any local stops. The location was perfect, especially for those taking their daily walks to stop right in. He smiled. Five years ago, he knew this was where he wanted to be, and he didn't want anything to change, which was what led to that fight with her.

"Morning, Mr. Javin. Gary."

"Morning, Tracy." He approached his secretary, who handed him a series of notes. "Anything important?"

"The usual. Weren't you taking today off?"

"Things changed." He looked around the spacious office and then at the large wooden desk that separated him from Tracy. He noticed nail polish and a nail file between her computer and a stack of unopened letters. He glanced up at Tracy, always thinking that she should become a model, but instead, she was his secretary. He smiled at her. "Just tying up loose ends." He walked into his office.

He hung his coat up on a rack by his desk and sat down in his leather chair, sorting through the notes that his secretary had given him. The usual clients. Nobody new. Not yet anyway, but that big case that he had just won should be opening more doors soon.

"Boy, you look like shit." Bill Henders stepped into Gary's office and closed the door behind him. The left side of his face was slightly bruised and scratched up. Wearing a black suit with a yellow tie, he took a seat in front of Gary's desk. "Thought you were taking the day off today?"

"I was."

"You were? Problems at home?"

"Nothing that could be fixed." He folded his hands in front of him. "How's Jen doing?"

"Recovering from the car accident." Bill touched the left side of his face. "You know, when we moved up here from the city, I thought we were leaving the roadragers behind, but we got him. And that bastard is now in jail for what he did."

"He picked the wrong guy to screw with."

"That he did." Bill played with the gold wedding band around his finger. His blue eyes were usually bright, but today, they looked tired. "So, why are you really here? The Randall case was a huge case. I thought you and Holly were going to leave town and celebrate this weekend." Gary frowned. "So, what happened?"

"She wants kids."

"That's great." Bill read the look on his friend's face. "But you don't?" Gary shook his head. "Gar, you're almost forty. If you don't have kids now, when?"

"I don't know." Gary leaned back in his seat. "Things are good right now. I don't want to change that. I don't want to change anything. I just want things to be left the same."

"You know what you need?"

"What?"

"A drink." Bill jumped out of his seat. "Come on. It's Friday. We aren't scheduled to do much business today anyway, so let's get a drink." He smacked his hands together.

"Bill, it's ten a.m."

"So?"

"So, how about we wait till lunch, and then we head over to Earl's?" Tracy knocked on the door. "Come in."

"I'm sorry to disturb you." She looked at Bill before saying to Gary, "I have your mother on hold. Should I take a message?"

"No, she probably wants to break my chops about surprising her for her sixtieth birthday." Bill laughed. "We got her good, and she's not going to let me forget that. Tracy, put her through."

"So, noon?" Bill retreated to the door. "Earl's?"

"Noon. Earl's." The phone rang. "Hi, Mom." He watched Bill follow Tracy to her desk, knowing that he was staring at her ass. "How are you doing?" A long pause. "I'm sorry. I forgot." He swallowed hard. "Yeah, I know. I know. Dad's been gone for two years now. I didn't forget. I mean… I did, and I'm sorry. I should've called. Are you okay?" He listened for a moment. "Holly called you. What did she say? I see. Look, I don't want to get into it. Can I call you later? Okay. I'll call you later. Love you. Bye."

He hung up the phone and ran his fingers through his brown hair. "Thanks, Holly," he muttered. "Just what I needed." He grabbed a note off his desk and dialed a number. "Hey, Mr. Bentley, you called. Your son's in trouble again? I see. Where was he arrested? He's being arraigned today? When?" He glanced at his watch. "It'll be cutting it close, but I'll try to be there. Yeah. Bye." He slammed the phone down. "Bill?" He hurried out of his office, moved past Tracy's desk, and walked into Bill's office. "Bill, I need a ride to the courthouse."

4

"What about our drink?" Bill was throwing paper balls into his wastebasket. "We have a date, right?"

"Mr. Bentley's son was arrested again."

"Jesus. What was it this time? Drugs? Assault?"

"Attempted Murder." Bill froze in mid-slam. "How about that ride?"

"Sure." Bill rose from his chair. "Earl's later?"

"Later."

"Okay. Let's go."

"Tracy, I'll be at the courthouse." They moved toward the office door. "Just take notes, but hold my calls. I'm done after this." He looked over his shoulder to see her nod, and he stepped outside with his partner and friend in tow. So much for a quiet day.

A drink did not fill Gary's hand until almost six. Tired eyes roamed around the cozy bar called Earl's. Everyone was always laughing and smiling here, especially the big man called Earl, but not Gary. He had to go home soon and face his wife. A roar of thunder made him jump, and he steadied the drink in his hand, then took a quick slug, enjoying the beer running down his throat.

"Long day?" Earl stood before him. He could've been a wrestler or boxer, but instead, he chose to open a bar in this town. His eyes were always sad as if keeping a dark secret to themselves, but his laughter rang like a bell from his heart. He was quiet but merry, and only occasionally did Gary see this man lose his temper, not a pretty sight. "You look like you had a long day. Problems at home?"

"My wife wants kids. I should be happy about that."

"But you're not?" Earl took a white dust cloth and wiped the counter between them. "Change is good, Gary." A roar of thunder almost made him jump, but he shook it off. "A nasty storm is coming. You should leave before it gets here." He walked away.

"A bad storm is brewing." A stranger pulled up a stool beside Gary. "Nature's a bitch, and she don't like to be cheated." He gestured toward Earl and pointed at Gary's beer. "Where's your friend?"

"What friend?" Gary knew this man was inquiring about Bill, who was outside on his cell phone, talking to his wife. "Can I help you with something?" He glanced at him and then realized that it was the same man from the bus ride this morning.

"No." He finished his beer and then dropped a twenty on the counter. "I came here six months ago, and I'll be leaving tonight."

"Okay."

"And you'll be leaving too." Gary froze in his seat. He could feel the strange man's breath touch his cheek. Was he threatening him? "Beware the storm, Gary." He backed away from him just as Bill walked toward them. "She's coming for you," and he hurried away, pushing past Bill and disappearing outside.

"What the hell?" Gary, more angry than afraid, spun around, staring at the door, where the man had exited. "Was that a threat?"

"Want me to call the police?" Bill watched Gary shake his head. "He looked crazy."

"Is that supposed to make me feel better?" Gary shuddered as if someone had just walked over his grave. "Crazy bastard. He told me to beware the storm.". He jumped from another crash of thunder.

"Well, he was right. It's a real bad storm rolling in, and I think we should call it an early night." Bill gestured to Earl for one last drink. "One for the road."

"You head out. I'm staying for a bit." Gary nursed his drink. "I can't go home yet."

"Come on, Gary. Just talk to her. You're good at that."

"I know, Bill, and we should be having fun, going away for the weekend and not fighting. I just don't want kids. Not now anyway."

"You might change your mind." Bill slapped his friend on the shoulder. "Whether you want it to or not, your life will change. Sometimes, we can't control what happens, and sometimes, we can." He finished his drink. "See you on Monday."

"See you on Monday." Gary watched Bill leave the bar. The lightning outside flashed, and the thunder roared. He would leave soon but not too soon. Remembering the crazy man's words, he muttered, "Beware the storm. She's coming for you." What the hell did that mean?

An hour later, Gary was dodging baseball-sized hail. He used his briefcase as a shield, but he was still drenched. It was late, so the buses weren't running. He grabbed a cab and was dropped off in front of his house, but instead of walking into the house, he went and sat in the car.

"This is ridiculous! Okay. You're sending me a message, right?" He stared up at the sky, and the storm answered with a wicked streak of lightning. "Okay. She's been acting strange for the last three months or so. I'll hear her out, and we'll come to some sort of agreement. That's right. We'll agree, and we'll forget all about this fight." He opened the car door and stepped outside. "Holly…"

An electric snap. His body tingled, teeth vibrated. His knees buckled, and the cold, hard ground rose up to meet him. His face smacked against concrete, and consciousness slipped away. But he fought to hold on, struggling to stand, and was able to run into the house.

The lights were out. No sign of life upstairs. Maybe she's out, he thought as he moved toward the couch. His mouth was dry, and his eyes stung. As he fell down into the couch, a knot turned in his stomach, but consciousness slipped away before he could think. The darkness consumed him.

A freight train running wild described the intensity of Gary's headache.

Splinters of light pierced his eyes. Movement caused motion sickness, and a whistling sound like a train speeding through a tunnel filled his ears. Gary knew that he did not have that much to drink, so why was he hung over?

"What the hell?" His voice was hoarse. "Holly." He ran up the stairs and walked into the bedroom. "Holly?"

Instead of a luxurious bedroom, an empty space met his gaze. The windows were bare and revealed a gray sky after a storm. The walls were chipped, broken, and the floor was the same. The closets were vacant, and the only clothes Gary had were the ones that he was wearing. He ran into the bathroom to splash his face with water and wake up from this nightmare, but the pipes snarled and groaned and refused to produce water.

"No," Gary whispered. "Holly, where are you?" He stepped out into the hallway. All the picture frames were gone. He moved down the stairs and back into the room where he had been sleeping. "What is this?" He saw no television set, no portable alarm clock on the floor, no coffee table, and no grandfather clock. All he saw was empty space and some furniture covered in white sheets. "What happened to me?"

Gary smacked himself across the face. Snap out of it, he thought, and he felt his pockets until he found his wallet. Everything was accounted for including his home address on his license, this address, so this had to be some sort of mistake. Maybe, Holly was messing with him and reached out to Bill to help her teach him a lesson, but why did they take everything away?

Gary stepped outside. The neighborhood seemed the same. It was a little quieter, but it was morning. He turned to close the front door when he noticed the EVICTION notice posted on it. "Nice touch, Bill," but he found it hard to laugh. The knot in his stomach tightened.

"Where's my car?" Gary stared at the vacant driveway. "Holly, Bill, you guys are not funny. They must've towed it while I was passed out." He sighed loudly. "Okay. I'll take the bus again, go to my law firm, and confront Bill. Holly will be there, waiting for me," but he did not believe his words. "She'll be there."

Like yesterday, Gary waited for the bus by the local convenience store. It was the same driver too, and Gary finally relaxed. See, nothing to worry about, he thought, but the knot in his stomach tightened again.

"Morning," Gary said, but the driver just glared at him. "How's your son doing today?"

"You trying to be funny?"

"No."

"My son's in prison."

"What?" Gary shook his head. "No, he's not."

"You want me to kick your ass?" Gary froze at the venomous tone. "I'll do it. I don't care if I lose my job. One more word about my idiot son…" He pointed a jagged finger at Gary. "And you're done."

"I'm sorry." The bus driver ripped the money out of his hand. "Don't you recognize me? You picked me up here yesterday."

"I don't know you, buddy. Now, get on or get off. I have a route to keep, and no favors. Get off wherever you need to and walk."

"Okay." Gary slowly moved past him and took a seat. He noted that the bus was almost empty unlike the day before. "No commuters today?" He quickly regretted asking that.

"Where do you think you are? Long Island?" The bus lurched forward, and the driver shook his head. "Some people," he muttered.

Gary knew it was a Saturday, but people were always riding the bus. They were mostly doing errands or heading down to the city. Then, he looked out the window, and his mouth fell open. The local stores were either closed, or they were chained up with bars on the window. An old man swept outside his bagel shop, but he was soon harassed by a bunch of delinquents. And nobody moved to help him. The bus rode on, passing demolished developments and real estate signs hanging broken, sprayed by graffiti artists.

"This is a nightmare," Gary said as he exited the bus. "This can't be real." The bus tore down Main Street. "This can't be…" Then, he saw it, the sign for his law office, but now it read: Henders and Brian Associates. "What?"

Stepping inside, everything looked the same. Tracy sat at the receptionist desk. There were two adjoining offices, and Bill was in his office. But who was the strange man sitting in Gary's chair?

"Can I help you?"

"It's okay, Tracy. That's my office."

"Excuse me, and how do you know my name?"

"Tracy, it's Mr. Javin. Gary Javin. I'm an attorney with this firm, and you're my secretary." She looked at him like he was crazy. "Tracy, you've been with this firm for almost five years now."

"Yeah, but how do you know that?"

"Bill? Bill?" Gary moved toward him. "Thank God, you're here. What's going on? What happened last night?" Out of the corner of his eye, he saw the other man emerge from his office, but Gary ignored him. "Bill, help me out here. What's going on? Why's the sign different outside?"

Bill sat at his desk with the Waken Herald in his lap. He stared out the window, touching his ring finger where his wedding band once was. He turned toward Gary, but he did not recognize the man before him. He wanted to curse at Tracy for even being bothered, but this man continued to stare at him intently like he knew him and like he had all the answers. But he didn't. He just wanted to be left alone. "Can I help you?"

"Jesus, Bill. Your face. Why is the right side of your face so bruised and scarred?"

"Who the fuck are you?" Bill jumped to his feet and now stood inches away from Gary. "Who do you think you are coming in here and saying that to me?"

"Bill, it's me. Gary. We had drinks last night."

"I don't know you." The man behind Gary took a step closer, but Bill raised his hand. "Get out, or you'll be thrown out."

"Bill, what is this? We won that big case last week. Remember? The Randall case?"

"I won that case," the other man said. "You weren't there."

"I was there," Gary snapped at him. "Please, tell me that this is some sort of joke, that Holly put you up to this. I mean… What would Jen think?" Bill punched him in the face; his blow sent him spiraling to the floor. "Bill! What the hell?"

"My wife died in a car accident." Bill towered over him. "Tracy, call the cops." Fear covered her face, and she didn't respond. "Tracy." She blinked and did what he asked. "Now, last chance, pal. Get out or get arrested for trespassing."

"Bill." Gary staggered to his feet. "Jen's alive." Bill moved toward him, ready to strike again, but the strange man held Bill back. "I'm sorry."

"Get out," the strange man yelled at him. "Get out!"

Hurrying outside, Gary paused by the curb. He turned to look at a condemned grocery store and an abandoned strip mall. The streets were broken, unpaved, and pedestrians moved fast as if their lives depended on it. What the hell happened, and he saw one of those bins for the Waken Herald. He dropped in a dollar, snapped open the lid, and pulled a newspaper out, and again, his mouth fell open. The paper was dated six months later from yesterday, but how was that possible?

For an hour, Gary wandered around Main Street. He had to duck into the alleyway once or twice when he saw a gang of delinquents walking in his direction. He didn't need to be mugged or beaten up, and in his reality, these were good kids. But the looks in their eyes said different, everything was different. The life that he knew, his wife, and his friend were gone. There was no going back, and he knew that the strange man from last night was right. He cursed himself for not believing him, but how the hell could something like this be believed? Was the storm really responsible for bringing him here?

There was no going home. There was no going to the office. Only the cold, hard streets and the run-down shelters, where some would not make it out alive was all there seemed to be around him. There was only one place left to go, one place that Gary prayed still existed. Hoping to be right, he hailed a cab, and he was. Relief flooded through him as he arrived at Earl's, which looked identical to where he was last night, a cozy, little bar off Main Street.

"Thank god…"

The door swung open, and Gary's mouth, which seemed to become a habit, fell open. Instead of brilliant lights, the place was dim. Warmth was replaced with tension, no laughter or smiles. Some men played pool in the corner like they did last night, and a few sat at the bar nursing their drinks. But the men sitting at the tables, whispering to one another, were not lawyers or doctors. They were more of the criminal type, and he recognized a few men who should've been locked behind bars. They all looked at him.

Moving fast, Gary headed toward the back where the restrooms were. He glanced at Earl, who returned his look, but he didn't smile at Gary. Earl looked the same, but was it really him? Maybe, this was a bad idea, but Gary remembered seeing a payphone once near the restrooms. He didn't have a cell, and if he did, it probably wouldn't have been working. Luckily, he had some change, and now it was time to find his wife Holly.

Holly's mother lived just outside of Waken. Holly visited her often and most of the time alone. Gary cursed himself for always working. She was trying to tell him something. She's been trying for the last few months or so, and he didn't want to listen. He wanted to win the Randall case, and he did. But the victory had cost him his wife, and now his life was gone. He needed her, needed to find her. Hoping against hope that she would be there, he dialed her mother's number.

"Hello?"

"Holly? Oh, thank god."

"Who is this?"

"It's Gary."

"Gary?"

"Yeah. Gary."

"I'm sorry. Gary? Do I know you from work?"

He looked at the phone in his hand. "Holly, it's me. Gary."

"Gary who?"

"Your husband."

"What?"

"Look, I know we fought, and I'm sorry. I'm so sorry, Holly. Please, forgive me."

"Look, Gary, you must have me confused with someone else."

"Then how did I know that you would be at your mother's house?" Silence. "Holly, how did I know that?"

"I don't know." Silence again. "But you're not my husband."

"Yes, I am." He gripped the phone tighter. "I am your husband, and I love you. I love you so much, Holly."

"My husband is here, Gary. He's sitting across from me at the kitchen table right now."

"What?"

"Don't call here again, or I'll call the police."

"Holly..." The line went dead. "Holly." He looked at the wedding band on his finger. "I have lost you." He wiped his tears away. "Mom," he whispered and quickly dropped in more coins, dialing another number.

"Yes?"

"Mom?"

"Hello?"

"Mom, it's me."

"Alex?"

"No. It's Gary. Who's Alex?"

"Alex is my son. Are you calling to speak to him?"

"No. Mom, it's me, Gary."

"I'm sorry, but my son's name is Alex. Who are you calling for?"

"Mom, you don't have a son named Alex." He didn't mean to get angry at her, but he had enough. "Please, tell me that you remember me, that you remember your son."

"My son's name is Alex."

"Mom, did you celebrate your sixtieth birthday recently?" He leaned closer to the phone and smiled when she said yes. "And you went to that seafood restaurant that you really like? The one with the boats?"

"Yeah. Were you at the party?"

"Yes, I was at the party."

"Okay."

"And you remember how you got sad that not everyone could not make it there?"

"No. Everyone I wanted was there."

"Dad wasn't."

"What are you talking about? He was there."

"Dad's alive?"

"My husband is alive. Look, what is this? What do you want?"

"I want you to remember me. I want you to remember your son."

"I have a son. His name is..."

"Gary."

"Alex." A moment of silence passed. "You must have me confused with someone else. I have to go. Thanks for calling."

"Mom..." The line went dead. "Mom..." He slammed the phone down hard.

"Hey!" Earl stood behind him. "You break it, you pay for it." He glared at Gary, who shrank back a little. "Understand?" Gary slowly nodded. "And only customers use the phone, so you better buy a drink before leaving." He poked Gary hard in the chest. "Got it?" Gary nodded again. "Good. No freebies here." Earl stormed away.

"Got it," Gary mumbled as he rubbed his chest. "Not the man I knew," he said, but then he remembered something. Taking out his wallet, he dug around until he found a business card. It was from a reporter who had dogged him about the Randall case. He lifted the phone one last time and called the Waken Herald.

Five minutes later, he was at the bar, nursing a beer. Nobody paid any attention to him, and he was grateful for that. All he wanted was to be left alone and to think as his mind returned to that stranger from last night. He knew. He knew something was going to happen, but what? His brow furrowed, and then he realized. "I was struck by lightning." He caught the look on Earl's face. "That's how I got here, but how do I get back?"

"You should never have come back," Earl mumbled, but Gary heard him. The big man didn't seem sad like his other self but angry, angry at the world. He was also nervous. His eyes darted around Gary and then returned to meet his gaze. "You should…" He froze as a man bumped into Gary.

"Sorry," the man growled. "Didn't see where I was going," but he looked Gary right in the eye. "Sorry. My mistake." He and his friend grabbed the table behind Gary.

Gary kept his back to the two men that now watched him intensely and finished his drink. "One more, and then that's it, I guess."

"Maybe, that is it," Earl said to him, but one of the men behind Gary shot him a dirty look. He cleared his throat. "On the house." He went to get Gary a drink.

"Something wrong," he asked, but Earl shook his head and moved away.

Marc sat back in his chair with his eyes burning into Gary's back. He gingerly touched the scratches under his chin. He thought of the hitchhiker he picked up and smiled as he remembered her screams and moans while he had his way with her. Good times, he thought, but the man at the bar was ruining that memory. The man at the bar wasn't supposed to be there, but he was. "Dell, you remember that guy who owed us ten grand?" His friend shrugged. "It was maybe a year ago."

"What about him, Marc?" Dell was a rough man with scars covering most of his body. A prison tattoo covered his right shoulder, and his knuckles cracked. Hating to sit still, he ground his teeth. The last thing he wanted was to come in here and drink. He wanted to do some damage, not reminiscence about old times. "What about him?"

"Well, he never came up with the money."

"I remember." Dell finished his drink and wiped his mouth with his arm. "I remember what we did to him," he whispered. "Why bring him up?"

"Well, he's dead, isn't he?" He leaned closer to Dell. "He couldn't have survived what happened to him, could he?"

"No way in hell, and I'm not following." He slammed his empty mug onto the table. The sound made those around him jump. "Are we taking a walk down memory lane or something?"

"No." Marc leaned back for a moment and then moved closer to Dell. "I was just wondering something."

"What?"

"If he was dead, then why is he sitting at the bar?"

"What?" Dell turned to look at Gary. "It's not him. Plus, I saw a wedding band on his finger. Our guy wasn't married."

"Our guy was a con artist, and it was a year ago. Maybe…" Marc moved closer. His face was inches away from his friend's. He whispered into his ear, "Maybe he survived, and he came back. He's here to rub it in our faces because he has our money, and we have shit." Marc leaned back in his seat. "Ain't that a bitch?"

"No. It's not him." Dell stood up and grabbed the empty mug off the table. "I need another drink." He moved away from Marc and then paused. "And a closer look."

Gary continued to nurse his drink. Suddenly, he felt that penetrating stare fall across his back, and it reminded him of Holly. He would never get to apologize or to hold her again. He was stuck here, and he didn't know what to do. He needed help. He needed a friend.

"I'm sorry, but you look like a guy with the weight of the world on his shoulders." Dell gestured toward Earl and then tapped his mug. He placed it onto the counter, and Earl scooped it up. Dell rubbed his chin and turned toward Gary. "Long day?"

"You have no idea."

"Try me." Gary realized he had this man's full attention. "I'm all ears."

"You ever find yourself somewhere that you don't belong?"

"All the time." Dell took a seat next to him. "You just make the best of it."

"Well, in this situation, you can't. It's like you don't exist or shouldn't be here. It's like you're already dead, but you just don't know it, So, how do you get back home?" Gary knew this man had no answers for him, but he needed answers. "How do you go back?"

"There is no going back." Dell knew Marc was right, but how was that possible? How was this man still kicking after what they did to him? He didn't remember him, which gave Dell the advantage, and he knew what Marc was already thinking. If he remembered them, then they were done, and he wouldn't let that happen. But how was this man still alive? "Have to get back," he said as he grabbed his drink from Earl. "Good talking with you."

"Same here." Gary didn't like the look on Earl's face. "What?"

"You shouldn't have…" He looked past Gary and at Dell and Marc. "Talking to him was a mistake."

Gary slowly turned around and looked at the two men. They returned his gaze. They seemed convinced of something, something that made his skin crawl. A sour taste filled his mouth. He glanced at his watch and realized that the day was almost over, and soon it would be dark. He would be alone, and those two men would be waiting. "Earl." He gestured for the bartender to step closer. "What are my chances of getting out of here?"

"Not good." Earl noticed the dangerous look on Dell's face and took a step back. "I could try and give you a running start, but that's all that you'll be given."

"Thank you."

Slowly, Earl filled two more mugs with beer. He steadied his hands and carried the drinks over to Marc and Dell. He placed one drink in front of Dell, and as he began to set the other one down in front of Marc, the glass tipped over. Marc flew out of his seat, giving Gary the chance to bolt, but as the two men realized what just took place, Marc slammed his fist into Earl's face. Earl fell to the floor.

"He's getting away," Dell roared, and he and Marc tore after Gary.

Gary was once a great runner. He did marathons back in college before he got serious about law. Now, his body complained as he moved, but he moved. And the two men gave up the chase. Gary ran until he couldn't run anymore and noticed that he had stopped right in front of the gates of the local cemetery. Without thinking, he walked through the gates.

A few minutes later, a car pulled up outside the cemetery. The ignition was cut, and two shadows emerged from the vehicle. They waited a beat and then followed in Gary's direction.

Crossing his arms across his chest, Gary looked at the tombstones that he was passing by. One tombstone caught his gaze. Gary fell to his knees, and a cry slipped from his lips. His eyes hugged the name before him, but how could it be? He thought that he didn't exist here, but then how could his name be on the tombstone? How could he have died a year ago today? "I'm alive," Gary cried. "I'm alive."

"Afraid not." Dell pressed his gun into the back of Gary's head. "You should never have come back."

"I'm not who you think I am," Gary screamed at him. "That's not me!" He pointed at his grave. "That's not me!"

"If that's not you…" Dell knelt down toward him. "Then, what? Who are you?"

"You wouldn't believe me."

"Try me. I'm all ears," Dell snarled.

"Dell, just kill him already. We don't need to be sighted by the damn police. Come on. Shoot him!"

"Hold on, Marc. This man should not even be breathing, but he is. And I want to know why. Who are you?"

"I'm a lawyer." Dell and Marc burst out laughing. "I'm from an alternate reality. You killed my other self." They stopped laughing. "You killed me."

"No." Dell stood up and took a step back. "I am killing you." He pulled the trigger.

"Finally," Marc exclaimed. "What the hell took you so long?"

"Because something's not right here." Dell glanced over at the grave. "He shouldn't be here, but he is." He shuddered at that thought.

"Well, maybe now he'll stay dead." Marc moved away from where Gary lay on the ground. "Come on. The police patrol this area, so let's go." He hurried away from the grave.

"He shouldn't be here," Dell muttered, haunted by his own words.

A tear rolled down Gary's face. His eyes remained open, staring at his name across the tombstone. A cold breeze rustled through his hair, and an image rose up in the last of his thoughts. Holly, and she was calling to him. He would find her again, somehow, someway, but not before falling into darkness.

## CHAPTER TWO

"Hello?"
"Holly? Oh, thank god."
"Who is this?"
"It's Gary."
"Gary?"
"Yeah. Gary."
"I'm sorry. Gary? Do I know you from work?"
"Holly, it's me. Gary."
"Gary who?"
"Your husband."
"What?"

"Look, I know we fought, and I'm sorry. I'm so sorry, Holly. Please, forgive me."

"Look, Gary, you must have me confused with someone else."

"Then, how did I know that you would be at your mother's house? Holly, how did I know that?"

"I don't know, but you're not my husband."

"Yes, I am. I am your husband, and I love you. I love you so much, Holly."

Brown eyes flashed open. Tears-stained skin. Lips, dry and broken, parted. A body ached, begging for no more pain, and hands reached for something that was now gone. Holly's mind replayed that conversation in her head over and over as she lay in bed. He was a stranger, someone, who believed that he knew and loved her, but she didn't know him. But she did. How was that possible?

"Holly?" Her husband stood beside the bed. "Are you getting up today?"

After the phone call, she couldn't look at her husband like she once did. She couldn't bear his touch. He was a gentle man most of the time, and he loved her. She had given up everything for him, everything that she wanted for herself, and now she didn't even want him. She wanted the stranger that called her, Gary, but why? Why did she feel this way? "I'm sorry," she heard herself say, but she wasn't. "My thoughts must've drifted off, Henry." She slowly turned on her side to face him. "Am I getting up today?" He slowly nodded, and his smile flickered. "Why should I?"

"Damn it, Holly." His smile faded. "You're thinking of him, aren't you?" He pulled the newspaper out from under his arm. It was today's copy of the Waken Herald. He looked at it for a moment and then threw it on the bed. "I know things have been hard, and your mother has been a great help, letting us stay here for a while. But it's time to get up. It's time to go home. It's over, Holly. Time to move on."

"No." She looked down at her wedding ring. "I'm still hurting, Henry." Her gaze met his. "It still hurts."

"Then, tell me what to do." He sat on the bed and reached for her hand, but she pulled away. "Holly, I'm your husband, not this Gary guy."

"I know that, Henry, and I don't blame you." She was frustrated and glanced at the newspaper. Something in the headline grabbed her attention. "What the hell?"

"Holly." She pulled her gaze away from the newspaper and looked at him. "Holly, I know it hurts, and there are doctors that you could see, doctors that could help you." He grabbed hold of her hand and squeezed it tightly. "I just want you to be okay. I want you to be my wife again like before."

"I lost the baby, Henry," Holly cried. "I lost her." Tears rolled down her cheek. "It can't be like before."

"It can." He moved away from her. "Before you know it, you'll forget about it. You'll forget about him." He sounded almost convinced, but his smile flickered again. "I have to go to work, but I'll be back early. I'll pick you up, and we're going home. That's final."

"If you say so," Holly muttered, her words making him pause by the bedroom door. "See you later."

As soon as she heard the front door slam shut, Holly sat up in bed and grabbed the newspaper. Pain stabbed at her stomach, and she doubled over. She let out a few jagged breaths and then relaxed. Leaning back into her pillow, she flipped to the article, whose headline grabbed her attention, "Man Dies Beside Own Grave." How was that possible?

What she did know for sure was that it was Gary, and he was dead. Her love was dead, but how could she love him? He was just a stranger, a voice on the phone, but there was a connection. She couldn't deny that, and he was gone. And so was her baby. She burst into tears. "Damn it," she cried. "Who the hell were you, Gary? Who were you to me?" She struggled to stop crying. "I have to know." She slowly made her way out of bed.

Still unsteady on her feet, Holly grabbed some clothes and forced herself to shower. She tried to wash herself clean, but she could still feel the blood. As she remembered the miscarriage, her legs ached, and her stomach twinged. With one hand against the wall, she finished her shower. She needed her strength to find the answers. She needed to know, and a few minutes later, she was dressed. She was ready.

Stepping outside, she was nearly blinded by the sun and raised a hand to shield her eyes, and the smell of freshly mowed grass filled her nostrils. She used to love that scent, but now it made her nauseous. Holding the car keys in her hand, she closed the front door, only to discover that her husband had taken the car. No matter, there was always the bus, and it didn't stop too far from her mother's house. Did she dare take it into that downtrodden town called Waken?

"Morning." A man dressed in plain clothes sat on the bench. He had today's issue of the Waken Herald tucked under his arm like her husband had done earlier.

"Morning." Holly sat beside him. She glanced at the newspaper. Remembering that headline she had read earlier, she shivered. She felt like death had walked over her grave and stole two loves from her heart. She missed the child that she would never know, and she missed him. Again, she needed to know why.

"Are you cold?" He removed his lightweight jacket, but Holly shook her head. He followed her gaze to the newspaper under his arm. "Here. I've already read it." He offered it to her. "It's okay."

"Thank you." Holly took the newspaper from him.

"My pleasure." The man glanced at his watch. He ran his fingers through his thick, blonde hair. "The bus is running late today."

"Really? I didn't notice."

"You going to Waken?" She stared at him, and he shrugged. "I work there, so that's where I'm headed."

"No. I mean... Yes." Holly looked away. "I have some business there. It's a horrible town, but I have to go there. Today."

"A lot of people outside of Waken are afraid to go there." Holly glanced at him. "It wasn't such a bad town once, but it fell apart. Who knows? In another life, it could've been a great town."

"I doubt that," she muttered.

"Well, it doesn't matter." He stood up and stretched his arms over his head. "The bus is here." He gestured toward the bus that made its way toward them. "It was nice meeting you." He held out his hand toward her.

"Holly." She shook his hand.

"Holly," he said. "What a beautiful name."

"Thank you." She looked at the newspaper and decided to leave it on the bench. It could provide only a few answers, and she had gotten what she needed from it. Now, she would take the bus into Waken and follow the clues given. She had to retrace his steps and to understand why out of everybody, he had called her. What was she to him? His wife or just a delusion? "Wait. What's your name," but the man had already taken a seat in the back. She preferred to sit in the front, but heading into Waken, she knew there was no guarantee that she would be safe.

Holly rode the bus through Waken. The man that she had met at the bus stop exited after the second stop. She wasn't sure where she should get off, but then she saw a law office with a sign reading Henders and Brian Associates. Something told her that this was where she had to go. "Stop!" She didn't mean to scream, but her heart was pounding. "Please, stop," she called to the bus driver, who growled in response.

"This isn't the usual spot, lady." He sighed as he looked at her. "I'll make an exception. One exception, but never scream like that again. Understand?" She nodded as he pulled the bus to the side of the road, and a car zoomed past them, slamming on his horn. "See what I mean?"

"Thank you." Holly exited the bus. "Thank…" She watched the bus take off down the road, but it didn't matter. She was here.

Walking into the law office, she was unsure of what to do next. She had come in here for a reason, but nobody was at the front desk. One office was dark, and the other had its door closed. She slowly made her way back to the front door but then stopped. She had come in here for a reason, and she wouldn't leave without one. Was he here? That led to a strong knock on the closed door.

"What!" Bill threw open the door, ready to tackle the one, who dared to disturb him, but he froze when he saw Holly. "Sorry. I'm sorry." His eyes were red, and his clothes were disheveled. "Can I help you?" He cleared his throat. "Miss?"

"Holly." She held her hand out to him, and he took it.

"Bill," he mumbled. "I'm Bill."

"Nice to meet you." She grimaced as her stomach twinged and almost doubled over. She realized that Bill was watching her.

"Here." He led her to a chair opposite his desk. "Can I get you anything? A glass of water? My secretary is out for the day."

"Water would be nice." Holly's throat was dry, and she cursed herself for falling apart. She would not fail or surrender and go home. She would do this. She had to do this. "Thank you." She took the glass in Bill's hand and slowly drank the water, ignoring the bitter taste.

"If you don't mind me saying…" Bill sat at the edge of his desk. "You don't look so well." Holly laughed in response. "What's so funny?"

"You're one to talk." Chuckling in response, he surprised himself that he could still laugh. "You look like hell."

"Well..." He grew serious. "My wife recently died in a car accident, and the bastard got away with it. I have an excuse. What's yours?"

Holly drank some more water before answering him. "I miscarried." She looked at Bill and saw the same pain in his eyes that she had seen in her own reflection for the past two weeks. "I lost my baby girl."

"I'm sorry."

"Don't be." She held his gaze. "We both lost somebody that we loved." She placed the empty glass at her feet. "Time heals all wounds? What bullshit. The pain just won't go away."

"I know what you mean." Bill scratched his fingers against the desk. "You want to forget, and you can't. It makes you miserable, angry, and nobody understands. They try to."

"And they don't," Holly said.

"No, they don't." A moment of silence passed between them. "I'm sorry for your loss."

"I'm sorry for yours." They continued to look at each other. "Have we met before?"

"No, but I was thinking the same thing. Anyway, what brings you to my lovely office?"

"I don't know. This strange guy called me yesterday. He was convinced that I was his wife." She saw a look cross over Bill's face. "You know who I'm talking about."

"Yeah, I do, and that's why my secretary called out today. She's all freaked out, and my partner thinks it's my fault. And I never met that guy before."

"He's dead."

"What?"

"That guy? He's dead. He was murdered yesterday."

"Jesus." Bill shook his head. "He must've been on drugs or something. What else could it be?"

Holly stared at her feet. "I don't know."

"So, Holly, you came into this town for what? What are you looking for?"

"I wish I knew, Bill, but I don't." Holly rose from the chair that she was sitting in. "At least, I know that I'm on the right path. He came here, but where did he go next?"

"Holly, you should be home resting." Bill seemed concerned, and she still felt that they had met before. "You shouldn't be here. In this town."

"I know, but I lost him."

"I thought it was a baby girl?"

"Yeah. I lost her and him, and he called me. He sounded so desperate."

"Holly." Bill stepped closer and placed his hands on her shoulders. "He

21

was on drugs. He was probably a criminal or con man. Go home. I'll call you a cab, and I'll even pay for it."

"No, Bill, you don't have to do that."

"I insist." He moved away from her and picked up the phone. "Please, Holly, let me do this for you. Okay?"

"Okay." Holly sat back down in the chair and watched Bill call her a cab, but she didn't want to go home. She didn't want to see her husband or leave with him. She wanted to stay. He had been here, but where did he go? Where would he have gone, if he were lost somewhere he didn't belong?

Bill hung up the phone. "The cab will be here soon. Just sit back and relax."

"Where do people go in this town? Is there a local spot?"

"Earl's," he answered, then he caught himself. "The people there are dangerous, Holly. I might work in this town, but I don't hang out there."

"I see."

"Go home, Holly." He sat back on the edge of his desk and watched her. "Don't go there."

"I won't," she said, but he didn't believe her. He still didn't when he helped her into the cab. "Take care," she said.

"You do the same." He paused for a moment and then slipped her his business card. "If you need anything or just want to talk, call me." She took his card. "Bye." He handed the driver a hundred-dollar bill. "Take her home." He walked back to his office.

Holly waited until the office was in the rearview mirror and then said to the cab driver, "Did you pick anyone up from that office yesterday?"

"Actually, yes," the cab driver responded. "Why?"

"Where did you take him?"

"How did you know it was a him?" Holly shrugged in response. "Earl's, but the lawyer said to take you home."

"I rather go to Earl's."

"Lady, he gave me a hundred-dollar bill."

"Then, keep the change." She stared up into the rearview mirror, holding his gaze. "Earl's."

"Yes, ma'am." He shook his head. "Here." He handed her his business card. "Call me when you had enough of being there." He saw a look of confusion cross her face. "I'll pick you up and take you home."

"Thank you."

"Don't thank me yet, lady." He drove toward Earl's. "You haven't even gone in there yet." As she pulled away from his gaze, he shook his head again. "I just hope you know what you're doing."

"I do," she whispered. The strength in her voice filled her up and silenced her knees from shaking.

Earl's didn't look dangerous. It looked warm and inviting, but Holly knew that appearances could be deceiving. She watched the cab drive off like the bus. Her sanctuary was gone, and there would be no white knights to come to her rescue. But she had to do this. She had to. She opened the door and stepped inside.

"What the hell?" He watched Holly walk into Earl's. "Is she crazy?" He sat behind the steering wheel and tapped his fingers frantically along the surface. "Eric, you're a fool if you go in there. Earl will be waiting for you, and so will they. Damn it, Holly! Why the hell would you come here?" Despite the urge to run in and save her, he forced himself to stay in the car. "She'll be okay," he muttered to himself. "She'll be okay."

Some men whistled at her. Others licked their lips. A big man wiped the counter by the bar, and he glanced up at her, almost sorry that she was there. She wouldn't waste any time. Moving toward the back by the restrooms, she discovered the payphone. This was where he had called her.

"Hello?"

"Holly? Oh, thank god."

"Who is this?"

"It's Gary."

"Gary?"

"Yeah. Gary."

"I'm sorry." Holly touched the payphone. She lifted the phone up out of its cradle and placed it against her ear. She said, "Gary?"

"Holly, it's me. Gary."

"Gary who?"

"Your husband."

"Hey!" Earl stood beside her, making her jump and almost drop the phone. "Another one," he spat as he stared at her. "The payphone is only for paying customers, lady. Buy a drink, or get out. I would rather that you got out." He continued to stare at her, and she slowly nodded. "Good." He stepped away.

"You said another one?" Earl froze in place and slowly turned toward her. "Was there a man making calls here yesterday?"

"You with that reporter?"

"No. What reporter?"

"Just go home, lady." Earl slipped behind the bar. "While you still can," he muttered.

"Wait!" Holly moved in front of the bar. "Please, I have to know. Was he here yesterday?" Earl began to wipe the counter down away from her, hoping that she would leave, but she stepped closer. "He's dead. He was killed."

The bar went silent. A look of fear crept into Earl's eyes. A few men, drinks still in hand, stood up from their tables, and others began to reach under their coats. Their eyes narrowed, and they watched Earl and Holly like hawks. One wrong move, and it was all over.

"Answer the lady's question, Earl." Dell leaned across the counter and winked at Holly. "Was he here?" Earl slowly nodded in response. "Was it her that he called?"

"Who the hells knows?" Earl said.

"Yeah. Who the hell knew that he had a twin?" Marc propped his elbows up on the counter and sat on one of the seats. "Hey, beautiful. You looking for a real man?"

"It wouldn't be you." Dell laughed at Holly's remark, but Marc snarled at her, flashing his teeth. "I just needed to know." She took a step away from the two men. Her stomach was already twisting into knots, and somewhere in the back of her mind, she could hear a scream. "Good day, gentlemen." Dell grabbed her by the arm. "I said good day."

"That would mean something…" Dell leaned closer, pulling her body against his. "If we were gentlemen." Holly stared at him, and he flashed a smile that made her blood run cold. "Are you with that reporter?" She shook her head. "Are you one of them?"

"One of who?"

"Dell, drop it," Marc whined. "The guy had a twin. That's all."

"No, Marc. He didn't, and no twin has identical fingerprints. Now, lady, are you one of them?"

"No," Holly cried. "Please. I just want to go home. I won't say anything. I won't tell anyone that I was here."

"Tell anyone what?" Marc saddled up closer to her.

"Nothing," but Holly knew. She didn't know how she knew, but she knew. These two men killed Gary, and Dell could see the truth in her eyes. But what was he asking her? One of who? "Please, let me go."

"Let her go, Dell." Earl's voice shook, but his fear was slowly being replaced with anger. "She doesn't know anything. Let her go." Dell shot him a look.

"She knows, so no, Earl. I can't let her go." Dell began to pull Holly toward the door, followed by Marc. "You're one of them."

"No," Holly screamed, but Marc pushed her forward. "No!"

"Call the police…" Marc spun around and stared right at Earl. "And you're a dead man, Earl." The door slammed closed behind them.

"Damn it," Earl roared.

"If it were me," one guy nearby said, "I'd call the police." A drink was thrown at his head. "I would, but I have to use the bathroom. Sorry, pal." He walked past Earl. "You're on your own."

"Fuck you! Fuck all of you!" Earl pulled a shotgun out from underneath the bar. He fired a warning shot at the ceiling that cleared most of the place out. "I've had enough of keeping silent." He pointed his gun at the men still sitting. "I had enough of the lies, the murder, and corruption! If only that damn reporter did what I tipped him off to!" His finger curled around the trigger, but the men took off. The man ready to use the bathroom bolted outside. "I'm done, you cowards. The bar's closed!" He pulled out his cell phone and dialed 911.

"Please," Holly cried as she rode in the backseat of the car with Marc holding her tight. "I just miscarried."

"Did you hear that, Dell? She miscarried." Marc licked her cheek. "Damn shame, but she's vacant now."

"Easy, Marc." Dell drove toward the cemetery. "She gets to see the grave first, and then you can finish her."

"My pleasure." He squeezed her right breast. His hand fell onto her leg, and he caressed her thigh. "My pleasure," he drooled, and Holly moaned in response. "You'll like me. I'll be the best that you would ever have because you won't again."

A few minutes later, Holly wavered before a tombstone. The earth was disturbed because the police had unburied the other body to be sure that it was the same man, and it was. Their rationality was a twin, but there were too many holes in that theory. Like Dell said, how could a twin have identical fingerprints when no fingerprints are ever the same, twin or no twin.

"He said it wasn't him. He said he was from an alternate reality." Dell held Holly's arm tightly in his grip. "He shouldn't have been here." He turned toward Holly. "Neither should you, so why are you really here?"

"Because he called me."

"Dell, let me have her."

"In a moment, Marc. I want to know. Some loon calls you out of the blue, and you put yourself in this situation because of that? Are you a fucking idiot?"

"I can't explain it, Dell." He flinched at her using his name. "I felt something when he called me. A connection. I was someone to him, and I needed to know."

"I see." He felt sadness at what had to be done, but if not done, she could turn the tide on him. "You know, don't you?" She nodded. "You know we killed him."

"Dell," Marc exclaimed.

"I know," Holly whispered.

"Then, you know what has to happen." He pushed her toward Marc. "Make it quick. She's suffered enough." He walked away.

"I know," Marc said. "Be quick, but I'll make her scream first." He threw Holly onto the ground and jumped on top of her. "Let's do it right here, so that Gary could watch." He quickly pulled his belt off and unzipped his pants. He then tore at her jeans, pulling them down. Just a few more moments, and he would be inside her. He would enjoy her like yesterday's girl, and then he would finish her. And just as he was ready to do the deed, something hard struck the side of his head. He fell to the side, unconscious, and Holly hurried away, pulling her pants back up.

"You okay?" A man stood before her, one that she recognized. "Are you okay?"

"Gary?"

"No. Not Gary."

"You're that guy from the bus this morning."

"Yes, I am."

"Have you been following me?"

"No, Holly, I just saved you." He held his hand out toward her. "I'm Eric. I'm a reporter for the Waken Herald."

"So, you're the one that they were talking about." She shook his hand.

"That would be me." He searched Marc's unconscious body until he found his gun. "These two men are bad company, Holly, and you proved my theory. They killed Gary Javin. Twice."

"You were listening to us? Why didn't you save me before this animal got on top of me?"

"Because I had to know." Holly slapped him across the face. "I guess I deserve that."

A bullet flew past them. Another struck a tombstone. Holly fell to the ground, and Eric dropped to his knees and fired the gun in his hand. A bullet tore into the ground before him, but his shot landed home. Dell fell backward, dead.

"My father's a cop." He stood up, lowering his gun. "He used to take me hunting." He turned toward Holly. "I'm sorry, Holly. I called my father before coming here, so the police are on their way. And I'm sorry for not being honest with you."

Holly walked up to him. She stood a few inches away. "Why were you really outside my house today?"

"Because he called you." Surprise filled her face, and her mouth dropped open. "I pulled the phone records from yesterday, and I spoke to Earl. He got nasty when these two showed up, and I realized that something wasn't right. Something wasn't right with these two men, so I was waiting outside the bar to tail them. I was just not counting on you to show up." Sirens filled the air. "Cavalry's coming."

"Thank you for saving me." She smiled at Eric and then turned toward Gary's grave. "He did call me, and I shut him down. I thought he was crazy."

"Did you believe Dell?"

"Dell asked me if I was one of them." Holly glanced at Eric. "Alternate reality? This isn't science fiction, but Dell's right. No twin has identical fingerprints, so how do you explain two Gary's?"

"He called me." Holly stared at him. "He knew things about the Randall case, things only the lawyers would know. He knew things about me like my favorite drink and sports team. I thought he was crazy too, and then Dell killed him. I got a tip this morning about it, but I wanted to see you first. I'm sorry for your loss."

"Thank you, but why didn't you say anything?"

"Because you're still in mourning." He fell silent for a moment. "We were something to him. You were someone to him." Tears ran down Holly's face, and Eric laid a hand on her shoulder. "You felt it. A connection." She nodded. " And you know that it can't be explained."

"I know." Holly was quiet for a moment. "I love him. I don't know how I could, but I do. When he spoke to me, I felt something, something that I never felt with my husband. Real love." She turned toward him. "I made a mistake, and my life went a different way. Maybe, somehow, we were supposed to meet, but I changed that. I never met him, and he found me. And now, he's gone like my baby girl."

"The question is, Holly, where do you go from here?"

"Home." She held his gaze. "Can you take me home, please?" He nodded. "Thank you."

A little while later, Holly showered again. Her knees shook, but another white knight had come and saved her. She no longer felt the blood, the pain, or the heartache. Determination pumped through her veins, and she felt strong. She got dressed again and stared at herself in the mirror. She was ready.

Holly's husband came home early. He found the suitcases waiting by the door. She greeted him and hugged him tightly, and he hugged her right back. Then, as he led her to the door, she pulled away, and his smile flickered.

"You were right this morning, Henry."

"Holly?"

"You were right when you said that it was over, and it was time to move on." She gestured toward the suitcases. "I packed your things, and now I want you to go."

"Holly." He stepped closer, but she backed away. "Why? What did I do?"

"It's not what you did, Henry. It's me. I don't love you. I don't think I ever did."

"Yes, you do, and I love you."

"No, you're in love with me. It's not the same thing, and I took the easy way out. I gave in and became your housewife, and that was never the life that I wanted for myself. So, good-bye, Henry." She gestured toward the door. "Thank you for taking three years of my life, but the rest is mine to live."

"Holly…"

"No! Get out. Get out!"

"You're crazy." Henry grabbed the suitcases and stepped outside. "Crazy bitch." He stormed toward his car but not before saying, "You'll be back!"

"No, I won't," Holly replied and closed the door. She turned toward the old, brass mirror that stood perfectly against its wall. She stared at her reflection, and the woman in the glass stared back. "I'm taking my life back." Her hand fell into her pants pocket, and she pulled out two business cards. One card was tossed onto the table in front of the mirror, but the other remained in her hand. "Bill," she said and smiled.

"Did I miss something?" Her mother walked into the house. "Was that your husband tearing up the road outside?"

"I told him to leave."

"You did?" Her mother held her gaze for a long moment. "It's about time." She walked past Holly. "He was never right for you from the beginning."

"Mom?"

"I'm glad you see that now."

To Holly's surprise, she laughed. She laughed until her sides hurt, and she turned toward the mirror. No more sadness met her gaze. Her eyes were tearing with happiness.

"Holly, you okay?"

"I'm fine, Mom." Holly looked down at Bill's business card. "I'm going to be just fine. Maybe, him coming here was meant to be. Thank you, Gary." She walked into the kitchen to see what her mother was making for dinner.

## CHAPTER THREE

He sat in the car, talking to himself. He looked up at the sky, at the storm approaching. A wicked streak of lightning flashed across the sky. Satisfied with his decision, he opened the car door and stepped outside, and she waited for him. They would not argue tonight but agree to disagree. She just wanted him home, and he was here, walking in her direction. And then he said her name, "Holly." A second later, he screamed, "Holly!"

Brown eyes flashed open. A body sat upright. Lightning lit up the room, danced off the coffee table, and flashed across her fear and grief. The grandfather clock ticked to her heartbeat, and a crash of thunder followed. Trying to press out the storm, she covered her ears, but it was too late. Gary was gone.

A shadow moved against the wall. She pulled the covers closer to her and tried to see through the darkness, but every time the lightning flashed, the shadow swiftly moved away. Someone was there. Someone was watching her. Was it him? "Gary," she whispered.

"Yes," he whispered back.

"Gary." Excitement filled her voice, but why was he hiding from her? "Where have you been? It's been six months."

"I'm sorry, Holly." He crept toward the wall and pushed himself into it. "Go to sleep. It'll be okay."

"Go to sleep?" Despite the storm raging outside, Holly realized that she was still really tired and found it hard to move off the couch. "Please, Gary. Don't leave me. Please, don't leave like that again. I thought... I thought you were gone for good." She fell back into a deep sleep.

"If only you knew," he whispered.

It was morning when Holly opened her eyes again. Someone was knocking on the front door. She slowly got up, and then she remembered. Gary had come home. Maybe that was him knocking, or maybe he had told Bill that he was back. Either way, she flew toward the door and threw it open, forgetting that she was only wearing a thin, silky nightgown.

"Holly!" Bill almost choked on his coffee when she opened the door. "It's cold outside." He pushed her back inside and closed the door behind him. "Maybe, you should get dressed."

"Bill, he's back."

"What?"

"Gary's back. I saw him last night." She looked around the house and wondered where he had gone. "I saw him during the storm last night. He was here, talking to me."

"Holly, calm down." He handed her the other cup of coffee that he was holding. "Are you sure that you saw him?"

"Yes, and I spoke to him." She didn't like the look on Bill's face. "What?"

"Well maybe, you had a dream."

"A dream, Bill? Really?"

"Holly, it's been six months. If he hasn't turned up by now..." He fell silent. "Maybe, you're right. Maybe, you did see him, and you spoke to him. So, where is he? Where's Gary?"

"I don't know." Holly looked down at herself. "You have a few minutes?"

"For you, Holly, I have eternity."

"Good. Then, I'm jumping in the shower, and I'll be down in fifteen. And if you see Gary, tell him that he is in deep water." She hurried upstairs. "Okay?"

"Okay, Holly." Bill shook his head as he finished his coffee, but then he realized that someone was watching him. He looked up and saw Holly's mother leaning over the banister and glaring at him. "Morning." She disappeared without a response, and a door slammed shut. "And good morning to you too, fine sir," he muttered. "Gary, where the hell did you go?"

Twenty minutes later, Bill drove Holly down to the police station. It had become routine. There was a detective still working the case, and he would give her the 411, if there was any. Lately, there was nothing, and she would leave disappointed. Then, Bill would take her to his law office, where she had begun to work as a secretary.

"I'm sorry." Detective Green looked up from his desk. "The case has gone cold, Holly."

"Meaning?" She wavered before him as Bill stared down at his feet. "What?"

"There are no leads to follow," Detective Green said.

"So, that's it?" She looked from Detective Green to Bill. "We give up?"

"I'm sorry." Pushing fifty, Detective Green was feeling his age, and he was tired. Hoping to find the lawyer, he had chased every lead, but most of the leads were dead ends. As time went on, the leads ran out, and the case became cold. He wanted to tell Holly to move on, to declare her husband dead, but every time he looked into her eyes, he saw hope. She wasn't giving up, but maybe, it was time that she did. "Holly, it's time. Time to consider that Gary is…"

"Alive. I saw him last night."

"What?"

"Holly." Bill shook his head at her. "It was a dream."

"No, Bill. It wasn't. He was in the house, and I spoke to him." Detective Green pulled out a pad and pen from his desk. "He was there, and then I went back to sleep." The detective took the pad and pen and placed it back into his desk. "He was there. Gary was there."

"Did you see him," Detective Green asked.

"Yeah. I mean… It was dark, but he was there."

"Holly?" Detective Green leaned back in his seat. "Did you see him?"

"No." Holly looked from Detective Green to Bill. "He was hiding from me."

"Why would he do that?"

"I don't know. You're the damn detective." Holly immediately regretted the anger in her voice, but the sympathetic look on the detective's face made her angrier. "You know what? Forget it. Just forget it. I didn't see him. Happy?" She glared at Bill. "I'm out of here."

"Stick around, baby," purred a man sitting handcuffed to a chair nearby. "I'll be the best that you would ever have because you won't again."

"Shut up." A police officer smacked him in the head. "You got your last girl, pal."

"Maybe." The man licked his lips at Holly. "Maybe not."

"Animal," Holly spat at him and stormed away, but she couldn't silence a growing chill falling fast down her spine. "What a pig," she muttered.

"Excuse me." She almost collided with a man, maybe early thirties with blonde hair, who was also walking out. "Holly?" They stared at each other. "I'm Eric. I'm a reporter for the Waken Herald." He held out his hand toward her.

"Nice to meet you." As she shook his hand, she noticed Bill was still talking to the detective. "Do I know you?"

"No, but I know you. I am… I was a friend of your husband, and I've been following his disappearance and the ongoing investigation, which I take is not ongoing anymore?"

"Are you following me? Is that why you are here?"

"No. My father's Detective Green. I just brought him lunch."

"Around the time that I'm here?" Holly held his gaze. "What do you want?"

"Answers like you, but the police still haven't found anything. They're giving up. Are you?" Holly shook her head. "Even after six months?"

"I wish people would stop saying that."

"I'm sorry, but at least…"

"At least what?"

"No body was found."

"Eric, that's enough." Bill pushed Holly away from him. "I told you at the hospital to leave her alone, but you just don't listen."

"Bill, I told you what I saw. Why won't you believe me?"

"Shut up!" Bill didn't mean to yell, but he did. "You didn't see him that night. End of story. Come on." He led Holly outside, ignoring the stare from Eric.

Bill got in on the driver's side and slammed his door shut. He stuck his key into the ignition and allowed the engine to rumble for a few moments. He looked over at Holly, who was lost in thought, and gripped the steering wheel with his hands. Slowly, he leaned back in his seat and turned toward her. "Holly," he said. "It might finally be time."

"What was Eric talking about back there? Did he see Gary the night that he disappeared?"

"He claims he did, but there's no way in hell that he did."

"Why not?"

"Because Gary came home that night. You know that. Look, Holly, if there was a chance that Gary was still alive, we would know it, but there's been no sign of him, no lead left to follow. It's time. You have to move on. I am. I have to interview people today to replace him. I have to interview this Brian guy, who I might consider, but I don't want to. I would rather have Gary back, but he's gone. He's gone, Holly." Holly leaned forward and turned the radio on. "Holly…" Bill fell quiet as he listened to the news.

"Local authorities are still stumped as to the disappearance of a crazed man six months ago during a vicious storm. The man had entered Saint Holly's Hospital and barricaded himself in a room, screaming to 'beware the storm.'

"Beware the storm," Bill gasped as he remembered the strange man talking to Gary. "Can't be the same guy."

"What?"

"As police stormed into the room, there was no sign of the man, but the window was broken as if struck by something. Police continue to investigate the strange man's disappearance and warn that he could be unstable and dangerous."

"Strange," Holly said, "but police are investigating his disappearance and not Gary's." As she turned the radio off, she noticed Bill rubbing the left side of his face. "Bill, what is it?"

"Um… Nothing." He switched the gear into reverse and backed out of his parking spot.

"You sure?" He nodded. "Now to your office?" He nodded again. "Good luck today."

"With what?" Bill asked.

"The interviews."

"Right. Yeah." He ignored the inquisitive look on Holly's face. "The interviews."

Holly knew there was something that he was not saying. It had to be about Gary. He saw him that night. Well, Earl too and some stranger, according to Bill. Gary had come home and sat in his car for a while. He was about to come inside when it happened. Closing her eyes, Holly tried to shake that image out of her mind. Instead, she turned to look out the window, and for a moment, she thought she saw him. She blinked, and he was gone.

"We're here." Bill parked the car. "How are you doing?"

"I'm fine, Bill. You've been a good friend to me especially with Gary's disappearance, but your wife might get jealous."

"It was actually her idea that I keep an eye on you."

"I have my mother."

"I know. I saw her at the house." He smiled. "I don't think she likes me right now."

"She does, but she's angry. I should be angry, but she is. Not me."

"He didn't leave you, Holly."

"I was thinking of leaving him." Holly was quiet for a moment, holding back her tears. "Look, it's been six months, right?" She watched Bill looked away. "He's not coming home. I want him to, and maybe, I did dream of him last night. But he's not coming home."

"So, what do you want to do?"

"Go to work, and you have your interviews. So, let's go inside. Okay?" She opened the passenger side door.

"Okay." He cut the ignition and watched her step outside. "Beware the storm," he muttered. "Why? What happened to you, Gary?" He got out of the car, straightened himself up, and walked to his office with Holly beside him.

"Good morning, Javin and Henders Associates." It still felt odd to say his last name with Gary being gone, but Holly did the best she could. "Hello." Holly heard breathing on the other end of the phone. "Hello? Can I help you?" The line went dead.

It was about noon, and soon she would be saying good afternoon instead of good morning. She glanced at her watch, a birthday gift from Gary, and as she stared at it, she remembered thinking she once had all the time in the world with him. Then, they fought, and he disappeared. She would never get to talk to him again, and that thought broke her heart. She shook her head and resumed typing a memo to one of Bill's clients. She wondered how the interviews were going. Would he really hire that Brian guy?

"I'm going to lunch. Want anything?" Tracy rose from her chair and stretched.

"I'm good. Thank you, Tracy."

"You have to eat something, Holly."

"I'll tell you what. When you come back, I'll go out."

"You'd better, or I'll bring you back a sandwich." Tracy looked at her long, red fingernails. "Damn, I chipped a nail." She moaned as Holly laughed at her, and then she was gone, giving a brief wave before closing the door behind her. Like with everyone else, Tracy was keeping an eye on her, which should've been comforting, but it was more of an annoyance.

"It's been six months. I'm okay. Why is that so hard to believe?" She shook her head. "My mother should also go back to her house, and everyone else should stop worrying about me. And I'm talking to myself." She jumped as the phone rang its shrill ring. "Good morning… Good afternoon, Javin and Henders Associates."

"Good afternoon." Her breath caught in her throat. "Hello?"

"Hello."

"So good to hear your voice."

"Who… Who is this?" It couldn't be him. It sounded like it, but it couldn't be him. "Can I help you?"

"That was some bad storm," he said. "Never seen anything like it."

"It was just a thunderstorm last night." Tears stung her eyes. "Nothing else."

"Not like six months ago." A long pause crept across her nerves. "I have to ask."

"What?"

"Why were you in the hospital afterward?"

"Holly?" She pulled herself away from the phone and stared at Bill. Tears slipped down her face, and her lips trembled. She didn't realize that she was pressing the phone so hard against her ear that it turned red. "Who's that on the phone?" Before she could answer, he pulled it out of her hand. "Hello? Hello? Who is this?" The line went dead, and Holly bolted from her chair. "Holly!"

Holly raced outside. The cold air smacked her across the face. How dare he call her after all this time? How dare he ask her that? She needed him then, and she needed him now. But he was playing a game of hide and seek with her. Why? Why was he punishing her like this? "You didn't want kids," Holly cried.

"Holly." Bill stood behind her. "Was that him?"

Tracy walked up to them, holding her lunch in a folded, white bag. "Everything okay?"

"Yeah." Holly tried to pull herself together. "I just need some air." She moved away from them.

"Holly, was that him," Bill asked again, but she didn't answer him. Instead, she waited to cross the street and walk over to the strip mall across from them. "Damn it, Gary," Bill muttered. "What did you do?" He glanced at Tracy and shook his head. "Just leave her alone. She'll come back." He didn't seem so sure, but Tracy walked inside. And he followed close behind.

The supermarket across the street wasn't as busy as it was in the evenings or weekends. The wagons were parked outside, ready to be taken and filled. The aisles were neat, stain-free with no yellow signs. Voices rose and mixed with music, but consumers were filled with thoughts. And she was focused on that phone call.

"Paper or plastic?" Holly looked at the man in front of her and cringed. "Which one?" Her eyes fell on his name badge, Dell, and she cringed again, sensing something but not sure as to what.

"Plastic. It's just a salad and drink."

"Plastic." As he bagged her groceries, she saw a strange tattoo on his upper left arm. "Prison tat," he said, "but that was a long time ago." He could tell that he was making her nervous, so he quickly totaled up her purchase. "$12.98." He watched her fish around in her pocketbook for her wallet. "I'm out of that life."

"Good." She finally found her wallet and pulled a twenty from it. "That's good." She handed him the money, wanting nothing more than to run away from him. There was something about him, something, but she couldn't tell what.

"Here's your change." He watched her hand shake as he gave her the money. "I'm Dell, by the way."

"Holly." She threw the change into her pocketbook, grabbed her groceries, and hurried away. "Thank you," but he just shrugged and began to ring up the next customer.

"Excuse me!"

Holly crashed into a man as she hurried outside. She fell backward, and her groceries tumbled to the ground. She heard glass break and didn't have to look to see the plastic bag filling up with juice. Her salad was probably ruined too. "Excuse me," but she knew it was her fault. It was all because of that strange man called Dell.

"Holly, we have to stop meeting like this." Eric leaned down and helped her stand up. "Are you okay?" He grabbed the soggy grocery bag, shook it a little, and then handed it to her. "Sorry."

"No, it's my fault." She took the bag from him and threw it into a nearby trash bin. "I wasn't hungry anyway."

"Let me make it up to you."

"Eric, is it?" He nodded. "Don't worry about it." She moved away from him. "It was just lunch."

"Then, let's go to Earl's. Take a longer lunch."

"Earl's? Earl's is a bar. Why would I go there?"

"He expanded, and it's now a restaurant and bar." Eric rubbed his chin. "You haven't gone there since Gary disappeared?"

"About that. Did you really see him that night?"

"Yes." Eric stepped closer. "I'll tell you more, if you have lunch with me."

"I don't know." She glanced across the street at the law firm. "I should get back."

"It's up to you, Holly." He stepped back. "Maybe, it would be better, if you didn't know." He moved away.

"Wait! Let me call Bill." She always forgot about the cell phone buried at the bottom of her pocketbook, but today, she remembered it. "Let me ask him if it's okay if I take a longer lunch."

"Just don't mention me. Bill might race across the street to kick my ass." Eric chuckled, but he also looked worried. "I told Bill that I saw Gary, but he won't believe me."

"Why not?"

"Because it doesn't make sense."

"Bill? It's Holly." The cell phone pressed against her ear. "No, I'm okay. I just ran into Eric." Hearing his name, Eric moaned in response. "Bill, it's okay. Jesus, calm down. It's okay. I would like to have lunch with him, and then he'll take me back to the office, if that's okay. Bill, it's just lunch. Okay?" Finally, she gave Eric a nod, but she didn't look happy. "I don't know who called before, and I would like to forget it. I'll see you in an hour. Yes, I'm okay. See you later." She closed her cell phone and dropped it back into the black hole that she called her pocketbook.

"Everyone's concerned about you, Holly."

"I'm okay."

"I told you not to mention me." He gave her a stern look and then broke out into a grin, which made her laugh. "At least, you can still laugh."

"Yeah," Holly said. "Now, how about lunch?" As she and Eric moved away from the storefront, she realized that Dell was watching them. "Why is he looking at us?" Again, she felt that chill falling fast down her spine.

Earl's used to be a cozy bar. The heavy, wooden door was still in place and creaked its welcome as people strolled in. The lights were dim, and people sat at tables or the bar, nursing their drinks. Behind the bar, there used to be storage, but Earl broke down the walls, expanding the place. Now, there were more tables and booths where people enjoyed meals and drinks, and the atmosphere was intoxicating. It made those inside feel welcome, feel like they were finally home.

"Holly!" Before she could react, Earl had her in a bear hug and squeezed her tightly. "I thought I would never see you again."

"Earl… I can't breathe." Holly patted him on the back, relieved that he finally released his hold on her. "Good to see you too." She gave him a peck on the cheek. "You've done an amazing job here."

"Well, I had to do something." He scratched the back of his head. "Eric." Earl gave him a hard stare. "You bothering her?"

"No, Earl. He's here with me."

"No hard feelings, Earl." Eric held his hand out to him.

"I don't know. After last time." He looked from Eric to Holly and then back to Eric. "Fine." He grabbed Eric's hand and squeezed it tightly, and the little moan that slipped from Eric's lips made Earl smile. "Come. Sit down. I'll give you the Earl's special." He led them to a table in the back.

Rubbing his hand, Eric muttered, "I bet you will."

As Earl walked away to get them their drinks, Holly turned toward Eric and said, "Okay. What was that all about?"

"Earl's brother." He pointed to a man's picture on the wall over the bar, a man barely in his twenties. "I did an article on a 1960's cold case, and the deceased was Earl's brother." He caught the dangerous look on Earl's face. "Anyway, you want me to tell you about Gary?"

"You know what? I don't know anything about you. Why don't you tell me a little about yourself?" Just then, Earl returned with their drinks, and Holly flashed him a brilliant smile. "Thank you, Earl."

"You're welcome," but his gaze remained fixed on Eric. "Your orders will be out soon." He walked away.

"How about Quid Pro Quo?" She glanced at Eric. "I'll tell you about me, and you tell me about you?" Holly nodded. "My parents were high school sweethearts, married right after graduation, and then I came along. My father joined the police academy, and three years later, my mother followed." A look of sadness crossed his face. "She died in the line of duty last year."

"I'm sorry." Eric gave her a brief smile, and she surprised herself by reaching across the table and touching his hand. "Why not become a cop like your parents?" She pulled her hand away.

"No interest." He took a sip of his soda. "So, how about you?"

"Me? I never wanted to be a cop."

"You know what I mean." Eric laughed.

"I know." She smiled as Earl brought over their food and then walked away. "I never knew my father." Eric froze in mid-eating of his hamburger. "My mother won't talk about him."

"I'm sorry." He wiped his mouth. "He left before you were born?" She nodded. "Your mother never remarried?"

"No. Instead, she attached herself to me." Holly poked a fork at her salad. "I just wish she could give me some space." She met Eric's gaze. "I know she's worried about me, and everyone else is too. But Gary didn't leave me. They just think he did."

"About that." Eric fell quiet for a moment. "I did see him the night that he disappeared."

"I don't see how. He was here, and then he came home. So, how did you see him?"

"I was in a car accident that night." Eric forgot about his food and focused on Holly. "I had the right of the way, and this guy was at this flashing light and didn't wait. He plowed right into me. The stupid idiot had his kid in the front seat with him too. Anyway, the police came and took the guy and his kid to the hospital. I didn't want to go, but the cops gave me a ride there anyway. And I was stuck in the emergency room for hours after that."

"What hospital?"

"Saint Holly's Hospital." He leaned back in his chair.

"If you were in the E.R., how did you see Gary?" Holly chewed on a piece of lettuce, giving him time to answer.

"I'm getting to that." Earl walked by, keeping his eyes locked on Eric, but Eric just merely shrugged him off. "I was sitting there for a long time, and then I noticed this strange guy nearby who was getting more and more agitated over the storm. He looked at me, and I swear to you, Holly, it was Gary."

"What?"

"He had long hair and a beard, but it was Gary."

"You're crazy."

"I called him, Gary, and he freaked out. It was like he didn't want anyone to know who he was. He ran into the E.R. and into one of the rooms."

"I heard this story, Eric. It was on the radio this morning." She pushed her plate away and wiped her mouth. "Maybe, this was a mistake. Maybe, Bill was right."

"Holly." Eric grabbed her hand, not meaning to hurt her, but to keep her here with him. "It was Gary." He let go of her hand. "I know something that the news didn't say on the radio this morning."

"And what would that be?"

"That he was struck by lightning." Holly's mouth fell open, and tears stung her eyes. "By your reaction, you know that I'm telling you the truth. You saw it, didn't you? What happened to him." Holly nodded as more tears fell down her face. "And he was gone just like the other one?" She nodded again. "But where did they go?"

"Holly." Earl almost stood on top of them. "Want me to throw him out?"

"Earl, relax." Eric looked from Holly to him. "She's okay."

"Eric, does she look okay? Why can't you leave Gary alone? Just leave him alone like you should've left my brother alone," Earl growled, not realizing that it was one of those rare moments when he spoke of his brother out loud. "You just don't know when to stop." He took a menacing step toward him.

"Earl, I'm okay." Holly wiped her tears away. "I'm okay. Thank you for lunch, but I have to go back to work. Can we have the bill, please?"

"It's on the house." Earl laid a hand on her shoulder. "Don't worry about it."

"No, Earl. It's fine. I can…"

"No," Earl said. "On the house. Want me to call you a cab?" He glared at Eric.

"No." Holly stood up from the table and surprised Earl with a hug. "Eric's taking me back to the office, but thank you. Thank you for being a good friend to me."

"I miss Gary," Earl whispered. "He was a good customer and a good friend." He hugged Holly and then stepped back. "Eric, take her back to the office."

"I will." Eric stood up from the table. "I promise, Earl." He watched Earl slowly nod and walk away.

On the drive back, Holly didn't say anything. Neither did Eric. Enough had been said, she guessed, and they both were lost in thought. Only they knew the truth about Gary, but Eric was right. Where did he go, and was he coming back?

"We're here." Eric pulled into the parking lot of the law office. "Sorry about lunch."

"I'm not," Holly said. "Eric." She looked at him for a long moment. "Do you think Gary is coming back?"

"Honestly, no." He held her gaze for a moment. "Do you think he's back?"

"I don't know."

"If he is, then you need to ask yourself something."

"What's that?"

"Which Gary is back?"

That question haunted Holly for the rest of the day. Sure, there were the regular office distractions. Phone calls, opening mail, and typing, lots of typing. Bill and Tracy also tried to ask her about lunch with Eric, but she remained vague about it. She just wanted to know the answer to the question Eric posed to her. Did her Gary come back, but how could there be more than one of him?

"Holly?" Bill was now driving her home, and six o'clock flashed across the car radio. "You've been distant since you got back. Anything I should know?"

"No," Holly said.

"Are you sure?" She nodded. "Okay. Same deal tomorrow? The police station and then work?"

"No." She noted the look of surprise on Bill's face. "I'm done with the investigation." He glanced at her, but she looked away. "If he comes home, he comes home, but I'm done looking for him. It might not be him anyway."

"What do you mean?"

"Nothing." Her house rose up into view. "It's like what you said. It's time."

"Only if you feel that it's time." Bill pulled the car up in front of her house. "We can still look for him."

"It's okay, Bill." She leaned over and kissed him on the cheek. "I'll see you tomorrow. Good night."

"Good night." Bill watched her walk up to her house. "Gary, did you finally come home?" He drove away, wondering if he would find his friend waiting for him tomorrow.

"Hello? Mom?" Holly opened the front door and then closed it behind her. "Mom?"

"In the kitchen, making dinner," her mother answered.

"Okay. I'm just going to run upstairs for a minute, but I'll be right down." She moved up the stairs, not hearing an answer from her mother.

The bedroom was dark. Lights flickered on and revealed an open window. The closet door was left open, and some dresser drawers were pulled out. If she didn't know any better, she would have said that someone had opened the window and gone through her things, but maybe it was him. Then, she noticed their wedding picture resting across the bed along with a white envelope that had her name on it.

"Dearest Holly, please forgive me, but we lived two different lives," the letter began. "I don't belong with you, but I love you. I will always love you, but I ask that you let me go. Never forget me. Keep me in your heart as I keep you in mine, but set me free. Don't look for me, and I won't call again. Let me go, Holly. I can't come back home. Love, Gary."

"Gary," Holly cried. "You were here. You were here." She looked around the bedroom. "If I had left you, I would've come back." She looked down at the letter in her hands. "You'll be back." That made her smile. "Maybe not now, but some day, you'll be back."

"Holly, dinner!"

"Coming," Holly yelled. She wiped her eyes and then folded the letter in her hands. She gently carried it down the stairs and left it on the kitchen counter near the sink.

"Holly, you okay?" Her mother noticed the letter and opened it. "Holly?"

"Don't worry, Mom." Holly moved toward a seat near the table. She bent down and lifted something up into her arms. "It's okay." She held something against her chest. "It's going to be okay. Right, Gianna?" She kissed her newborn on the head, and the baby laughed. "Mommy's here, and Daddy will be back."

12

## CHAPTER FOUR

Little yellow stars broke the darkness, shattering fear and holding to hope. Silver linings hung along spires, majestic buildings that dared to touch the sky. Clouds rolled in, hungry and omniscient, and lightning flashed in the distance. A car came flying around the bend. A sign rose into view, reading, "Now Leaving the City of Waken."

A gold pocket watch flipped open and closed. A hand tightened around it, and a woman's face flashed into view. A moment later, the watch resumed opening and closing, and a fist struck a leg. Red spots decorated clothing, and dirt covered his shoes.

"I can't believe you killed him."

"Don't start, Gary."

"Dell, how could you kill him?"

"Marc was in the wrong place at the wrong time." Dell continued to drive down the road. "We need to get out of this city."

"We didn't get the money."

"No thanks to Marc, which is why I killed him." Dell glared at Gary, who continued to flip his pocket watch open and closed. "Will you stop that? She's dead." The watch slammed shut. "She's not coming back."

"Fuck you."

"Fuck me? No, fuck you." Dell grabbed the pocket watch out of Gary's hands and threw it out the open window. "Fuck her. She ruined a good thing."

"No!" Lunging at Dell, Gary grabbed the steering wheel, and the car did a one-eighty across the road before slamming into a billboard sign. "No!" Gary ripped off his seatbelt and flew out of the car. "Where is she?" He saw the hint of gold and made a mad dash for it. "There you are!"

"She's dead, Gary!" Dell fell out of the car, spitting blood on the ground. "You watched her die!" He staggered to his feet and leaned against the large pole that led upward to the billboard sign. "Either way, she had to die," he muttered. He stepped back and looked up at the man on the sign, Bill Henders, who pointed at him and said, "I want to take you to court." Dell laughed and spat more blood on the ground. "I'll see you in hell, Bill!" He pulled his gun out of its holster. "She ruined a good thing," he said. "I guess this partnership has reached its end."

Gary ignored him, which he knew was a mistake. His heart was still breaking, and he held the pocket watch in his hand, wishing that she were still alive. The skies opened up, echoing his pain and misery, and lightning seared across the sky. A storm was brewing, one that made him cringe, but he remained on his knees, crying silently. And Dell's gun pressed against the back of his head.

"Ready to see her again?" Gary nodded. "I have to know. Did you really love her?" Gary nodded again. "Then, I envy you, but only one of us is walking away." His finger curled around the trigger. "I guess all good things do come to an end."

Lightning struck the ground and sent both men spiraling backward. Gary clutched the pocket watch, and Dell refused to drop the gun. Gary jumped to his feet and bolted, but Dell stood up and positioned the gun across his arm. Thunder roared like Gary's heart, and lightning flashed with the intensity in Dell's eyes. A bullet screamed, and it landed home, burying itself into Gary's back. Dell smiled a smile that would make your blood run cold.

"Gary…" Just as he took a step toward him, ready to finish the job, lightning struck the ground. "Jesus Christ!" Dell watched Gary lift up off the ground and vanish into thin air. "What the hell just happened?"

Darkness. Pain. Numbly, he slipped the pocket watch into his pants pocket. He tried to open his eyes. He tried to talk, but all he heard was a car screeching in response. More darkness. More pain. Finally, he saw light, a bright light shining into his eyes, and he heard a voice say, "What do we have here?"

"Not sure, doc. The driver of the car said that he just fell out of the sky, but look here. Someone shot him in the back. He's been in and out of consciousness, and his heartbeat is erratic."

"He's losing too much blood. Take him up to the O.R. Jesus, what the hell is going on outside?"

"It's a real bad storm, doc. It just came out of nowhere," the E.M.T. said.

"Gary!" He flinched at hearing his name. "Gary! Stop! Where are you going?"

"Sir, you can't go in there! Sir! Someone call security!"

"Gary!"

As he felt himself wheeled away, he struggled to open his eyes. Lights flashed overhead, and a searing pain engulfed his head. His hands shook, and his body trembled. His nerves were screaming, and his mouth was dry. He struggled to touch his pocket until he finally felt the outline of his pocket watch. She was safe, but he wasn't. And Dell would find him, if the police didn't first. As he struggled to think of an escape, he heard a scream, a scream that he recognized. It was as if he had been struck by lightning, and he screamed in response.

Darkness. Time slipped by, dancing to the beat of the heart monitor. An IV dripped, and a needle slipped into a vein by one of the nurses to draw some more blood. Footsteps echoed in the hall, and a Code Blue rang out across the speaker system. Voices drifted by with strange conversations. Someone called Waken a town, but Waken was always a city, his city. And he had almost run away from it because of Dell.

Gary cursed himself for that. He had met Dell in prison, and he allowed himself to become his friend, his partner. Then, Marc came along, and then Holly. Pain stung his heart, but it was the pain of losing her. Maybe, he should've died. Instead, he was here, playing the waiting game. Who would come first? The police or Dell? He hoped it was Dell because he would be damned before he'd go to prison again. Maybe, Dell was already here, watching and waiting, and then he would feel that pillow press against his face. Maybe then, he would see her again.

"Hello?" Gary struggled to open his eyes. "Hello?" His focus was blurry, but then a tall, Asian woman with short, black hair came into view. "There you are. Glad to see that you are still with us."

"What?" Gary's voice was hoarse, and his throat was dry. "What day is it?"

"Tuesday." She placed a cup of water into his hands, and he downed it in a heartbeat. "You've been in and out of it for some time now, but you're a lucky man."

"Thank you."

"Do you have a name?" He broke eye contact with the doctor, and his gaze moved over to the window. "I'm Dr. Wong." She pulled up the blinds to reveal the outside world.

"Where the hell am I?" Gary gasped.

"Waken."

"No. Waken is a city."

"No, it's a town." She checked his vitals, taking his blood pressure first and then sticking a thermometer into his mouth. "You lost a lot of blood, but you made it. And you picked one hell of a night to be shot in the back." She looked up at the heart monitor and noted his heart rate and blood pressure. "Your vitals are good." She discarded the thermometer and folded up the blood pressure cuff. "The police were here, but I sent them away."

"The police?"

"Yeah, but they'll be back." She was a quiet for a moment. "Who shot you in the back?" He didn't answer. "It almost shattered your spine, but lucky for you, the bullet missed it by a few inches." She held her index finger over her thumb. "You need to tell the police what happened."

"Can I recover first?" Doctor Wong nodded. "My watch? Where's my pocket watch?" She pointed toward the closet opposite the hospital bed, and he sighed with relief. "She's safe."

"She? Your watch is a girl?"

"Yeah. Long story."

"So, you're not going to tell me your name?" She sighed, but it was more of annoyance than relief. "Do you at least have insurance?"

"Yes, I do."

"Okay. Then, we won't have a problem. Now, come on. Sit up."

"What?"

"You've been lying in this bed for days. You need to walk around."

"Doc, I was shot in the back."

"And you're healing nicely, but not by lying on your back. Don't make me carry you." He laughed at her serious expression, but she finally cracked a smile. "It's a short walk. Doctor's orders."

"In that case." Gary struggled to sit up, but pain seared across his back. He tightened, muffling a scream, but she saw right through it. And with her help, he finally got out of the bed and onto his feet. "Thank you."

"You're welcome." She watched him touch an ugly scar that ran from under his right eye down to his chin. "That's a bad scar. What happened?"

"Bar fight." He shuffled forward. "A long, long time ago." He struggled to reach behind him to keep his gown closed. He didn't like feeling exposed or vulnerable, but right now, he was both. "Do you have another gown?"

"Sure." She opened the closet door, where he spied his pocket watch on the top shelf. She pulled out another gown and helped him put it on. "Better?" He nodded, but he still felt vulnerable. "Come on. Take one step at a time, and we'll do a short walk. And then back to bed, but you have to lie on your side."

"Okay," Gary said.

Gary kept his head down as they walked around. He couldn't take any chances of anybody recognizing him. Then, Doctor Wong stopped him in front of the nurses' station. She spoke quietly to another nurse, and he waited. His body felt weak, and he realized that the doctor was talking to him.

"I need your wrist." He looked down at the medical bracelet wrapped around his left wrist and almost laughed. John Doe was his name, and that was perfect. He held out his wrist for her to check the bracelet. "So, name?"

"Is that him?" a nurse whispered to the doctor.

"It can't be him," the doctor whispered back, but he heard her. "He didn't have a scar."

Gary was going to ask what they were talking about, but then he saw someone who shouldn't have been there. It was big shot, Bill Henders, who avoided public places unless serving a subpoena. What was he doing here? Noticing that the doctor and nurse were still conversing, he followed Bill Henders, curious as to why he was here in this place, and then he saw Bill Henders enter a patient's room and kiss someone on the forehead. It was Holly. "Oh my God," Gary exclaimed. "Holly!"

"Hey, you can't wander away like that." Dr. Wong saw the look on his face and followed his gaze over to that patient's room. "Do you know her?" He nodded. "That's Holly Javin."

"Javin?"

"Yeah. Her husband went missing recently. It's interesting that... Never mind."

"What?"

"It's interesting that you look like him, but he didn't have a scar." She shook her head. "Anyway, do you want to say hello?" Now, he shook his head. "Okay. Let's get you back to your room."

"Doc, about my stitches. When do they come out?"

"They don't. They're dissolvable."

"Good to know," he said, and she gave him a quizzical look. "I'm tired."

"Let's head back then," and she led the way. "Oh, maybe today or tomorrow, you could fill in some paperwork?" He nodded. "Good, and tomorrow afternoon, try to take another walk. You could walk with a nurse, if you want to." He nodded again. "Okay, and after tomorrow, I have to call the police. Okay?"

"Okay," but a plan was already forming inside his mind. "Holly," he whispered to himself. "That's why I'm here." Tomorrow afternoon, he would take a walk. He just wouldn't come back, and his doctor would find his bed empty. But that was only the first half of his plan.

It had been easy to sneak into another patient's room and steal his clothes including a baseball hat, which fit perfectly over his head. No security guards were seen patrolling, and the elevators were filled with doctors, nurses, and patients and their families. He mingled in and took the elevator down to the lobby where he exited into a waiting cab.

"Where to," the cab driver asked.

"What's the local hang out spot here?"

"Earl's."

"Never heard of it, but take me there." He checked the wallet that he had stolen and smiled at the cash inside. They always warned patients never to keep their valuables in a hospital, but this guy had not listened. Gary pulled out his pocket watch and flipped it open. "Holly." He stared at the woman's face. "I found you again, and this time, I'll do it right."

Earl's. The bar reminded him of that old show with the guy that later became Frasier. The bartender was far from beautiful, and he was tough. No bar fights, Gary reminded himself as he pulled out a twenty.

"What it be?" Earl cleaned a glass behind the bar before looking up at the man now seated before him. "Gary?" The man flinched but didn't respond. "Sorry, pal. You look a lot like a friend of mine, but no scar." He pointed to Gary's face. "So, what it be?"

"Beer." Gary dodged a bullet there, but obviously, the other him came in here a lot. He pulled the hat down further and then looked up to see a picture hanging over the bar. He stared at the man barely in his twenties, and he realized why the man looked so familiar. "Bobby?"

"What!" Earl slammed the beer down hard in front of Gary. "What did you just say?"

"That's Bobby." He pointed at the man's picture. "Is he here? Can I talk to him?" Earl looked like he wanted to kill him, and Gary realized something.

"He's dead," Earl said harshly.

He swallowed hard at the look on Earl's face. "Of course, in this world, Earl lived, and Bobby was murdered." He paused for a moment. "I'm sorry for your loss."

"You can't know my brother," Earl nearly spat into his face. "He was killed when you had to be a child."

"Did they ever catch the guy that did it?"

"No." Earl moved away from him. "You read that damn article in the Waken Herald?"

"The Waken Herald?" He was almost amused that in this world that damn newspaper still existed. "No," he said.

Rubbing his chin, Earl debated kicking this man's ass, but he had a reputation to uphold. "Finish your beer," he snarled. "Then, get out." He moved away but not without another nasty look back.

Gary sighed, letting the air escape from his chest, but he was sad. His friend was gone, leaving him with nobody here to trust, not even Holly. She might be the same woman that he knew and loved, or she might not be. He would've been happier with Bobby, who had drinks with him several times at his bar, but his friend was gone. He recalled that one night when Bobby confided in him and told him his deepest and darkest secret. He had hunted down the man that had killed his brother, Earl, and that man came from a wealthy family. He tried to pay Bobby off, but Bobby crushed his larynx instead.

"You have a pen?" Earl glared at him before he gave him a pen and the bill. "You called me Gary before." He started to write on the bill.

"So?" Earl now looked down at the bill, wondering what this strange man was writing.

"So, is that the guy who disappeared?"

"Yeah."

"I heard his wife was in the hospital."

"Holly?" Gary flinched at her name. "Is she okay?" Earl took a step forward, now staring at him intently. "Is she okay?"

"I don't know."

"What hospital?"

"I don't know."

"You don't know?"

"No. I don't know." Gary handed him the bill. "But I do know who killed Bobby," he whispered.

"What?"

"Be careful. He's slippery."

"You're crazy."

"No, I'm not." Gary moved away from the bar. "Bobby's favorite movie is 'Twelve Angry Men.'" Earl's mouth dropped open, and tears stung his eyes. "And he hated 'The Catcher in the Rye.'" Earl looked like he was about to break into a million pieces, and Gary almost felt sorry for him. But Bobby was his friend not Earl, and his friend was gone. "That's the man that you want." He pointed at the bill. "Not me."

"Who the hell are you?" Earl cried.

"Someone who doesn't belong here." Gary left the bar with those words hanging in the air behind him. "Someone that found her again," he whispered.

It didn't take long to hail another cab, but now he needed another destination. "Does Bill Henders work in this town?"

"What? Hey, pal, do ducks quack?"

"I guess that answers my question. Can you take me to his office?"

"Sure," the cab driver said, but he shook his head.

"What about Gary Javin?"

"What about him? The guy just vanished into thin air. The police are investigating, but they're not finding him."

"Was he a good guy?" Gary stared up at the rearview mirror, meeting the driver's gaze. "Was he a criminal?"

"Dude, what are you on?"

"Me? Nothing." He couldn't help but laugh as he sat back against his seat. "I just escaped from an alternate reality."

"Gary Javin is a hero to some, but to most, he's a lawyer. And he's a damn good one." The cab driver waited for another stupid comment or question, but the man in the backseat remained quiet. "I heard his wife was in the hospital."

"Do you know why?"

"No idea, pal, but I hear she's getting released soon."

"What's near the law office?"

"A shopping center," the driver said with heavy sarcasm. "Want to go shopping?"

"Yeah," Gary responded. "Take me there instead."

"Whatever you say, pal," said the cab driver, who was already itching to get this loon out of his car. "We're almost there."

"No tip for you," Gary muttered, but he already knew that the cab driver wouldn't care as long as he got out of the car. "Must be me," Gary muttered, "and my star reputation."

Once at the grocery store, Gary watched the cab fly off into the distance. He looked around at the other stores, which were typical for a shopping center. He saw a hardware store, pizzeria, deli, Chinese take-out, movie theater, and ice cream parlor. The grocery store was one of those super chains that you could get lost in, and right across the street was the law office with a sign reading Javin and Henders Associates. "I'm partners with big shot, Bill Henders," Gary gasped. "How did I get so lucky?"

A Jeep Liberty pulled up in front of the law office. Sure enough, Bill Henders, who only in his reality would drive a Mini Cooper, stepped out, and a moment later, an unmarked police car pulled up beside him. Bill Henders spoke to a man in plain clothes and then led him and the man's partner inside. Gary knew it was about him. Well, about the other Gary, but the sad truth was that they would never find him. And if that poor bastard was lucky, neither would Dell.

"Got a light?" Gary froze, recognizing that voice. "Hey, you got a light?"

"No." Gary swallowed hard and slowly turned around. He stared at Dell, who stood only an inch or two away, and he took a step back. "I don't smoke. I never did."

"Shame for you." Dell reached behind his back, and Gary remembered that was always the place, where Dell kept his gun. He liked having it press against his back, knowing that it was there, and ready to be used. "Relax," Dell said to him as he pulled a packet of matches out of his back pocket. "It's just matches." He lit his cigarette, shook the match till the flame disappeared, and then dropped the little, burnt stick to the ground. "Do we know each other?" He blew smoke toward him. "I think I know you."

"No, you don't."

"Don't I?" Dell stared hard at him for a moment. "Maybe, in another life." He smiled, but Gary remained standing rigid and wanted nothing more than to run away from him. "Speaking of which." He checked his watch. "Smoke break is almost over." His eyes moved from the watch to Gary. "What are you doing?"

"Nothing."

"It doesn't look like nothing." Dell looked over at the law office. "That lawyer over there disappeared. Poof, into thin air, but the cops won't find him."

"What makes you think so?"

"The guy put a lot of my old buddies away, and if any of them got out, they would look for ways to make him disappear. Maybe, they did."

"But not you?"

"Not me. I'm out of that life." Gary looked surprised, and Dell caught that look. "Do me a favor?"

"What's that?"

"Don't come back here again." Dell stepped toward the entrance of the supermarket but stopped to give him that look, that look of warning. "You understand me?" Gary slowly nodded. "I don't know what I ever did to you, but I get the feeling that you were looking for me. Are we done here?"

"We're done, Dell." Now, Dell looked surprised, and Gary realized that he never gave Gary his name.

"So, we do know each other." Dell flicked his cigarette on the ground where it landed almost on Gary's sneakers. "Now, get out of here. I've already put too many people in the ground, and I'm trying to stop. You understand me? I don't want to be that guy again."

"And you won't," Gary said. "You won't."

"Let's hope so." Dell retreated back inside, and again, Gary let out another deep sigh of relief.

"Shit," Gary cursed at himself. "That was close, Gary. Too close."

Gary didn't waste any time after that. He moved toward the law office and paused only when the cops came out. He stood a distance away, trying to hide himself next to a lamppost as Bill spoke to them, and the cops left.

Bill walked back inside but not without glancing at him first, but he shrugged off whatever thought came into mind. Now, the coast was clear, and Gary crossed the street. He waited a moment, surveying the area and looking for possible witnesses, but he saw nothing. Quickly popping open the back of Bill's car, Gary half expected the alarm to go off, but it didn't. He was a lucky man today especially with his encounters with Earl and Dell. He slid into the cargo area and closed the door.

Hours drifted by, and Gary fell asleep. He opened his eyes when the car shook. It was dark, late, and Bill had gotten in on the driver's side. A soft chime echoed throughout the empty space, and a cell phone lit up the darkness. Bill checked his rearview mirror, allowing the cell phone to ring once more, and then he answered the call.

"Hello? She's home? Good. Good. How is she?" Bill sighed. "No, they haven't found him yet, but they're looking. They're looking. You want me to come home? Okay. Okay. I'll check on Holly first, and then I'll be home. Yeah. I'll see you later. Jen, don't cry. They'll find him. I'm sure that they'll find him. Yeah. I love you too. Bye." Bill closed his cell phone and dropped it into a cup holder. A moment later, he punched the steering wheel. "Damn it! Don't cry, Bill. Do not cry." He started the ignition. "They'll find him. He's alive, and they'll find him."

"No, they won't," Gary whispered.

Gary could feel the car pull out of its parking spot. He continued to lie perfectly still, keeping his breathing low. He knew after seeing Bill in the hospital with Holly that he would lead him right to her, and he was taking him there now. He had no idea what he would do once they got to her home, but he would cross that bridge later. He just wanted to see her. She sounded like she was okay, but she did just lose her husband. She was also in the hospital, and nobody had said why. Was she sick? Was she dying, but he couldn't go through that again. Just let her be okay, he thought. Let her be okay, and he reached into his pocket and folded his hand over the pocket watch.

Time passed quickly, and the closer the car got to its destination, the more Gary's heart raced. The car parked, and he almost let out a shout of happiness. He caught himself, clamping a hand over his mouth, but Bill heard something. He paused before pulling the keys out of the ignition, and he stepped outside. A shadow fell across the back of the car, and Gary knew that Bill was just about to open the door.

"Bill?" His hand rested on the handle, but he turned toward the voice. It was Holly's mother. "Bill, come inside. We need to talk."

"Be right there." He stared at the car door for a moment and then laughed. His imagination was working overtime, and he was on edge. He thought he heard something, but it was probably nothing. "How's Holly doing?" He now stood by the front door with Holly's mother.

"Not good," she sobbed, and Bill hugged her. "I'm scared."

"I know. Let's go inside and see her." He walked Holly's mother into the house. "It'll be okay." He closed the door behind them.

Again, Gary wasted no time. He exited the car and slammed the door closed. Just in time because now Bill pushed the alarm on his key chain, and headlights flashed at Gary, angry at the intrusion. Another moment later, and Gary would have set that alarm off. Then, he would have to run, but not now. He walked toward the house, looking for a way in.

In the back of the house was a sliding glass door that led out into a green, spacious yard with a half-built patio. He saw a covered barbecue grill and some baseball bats leaning next to the house. Baseball bats? Really? What was he? A lawyer or a jock, but that didn't matter now. That Gary was gone, and he was the one that was left. He tested the glass sliding door and was pleased that it had been left unlocked.

Once inside the house, he paused, listening to the voices that came from above him. Now, he needed somewhere to hide, but where? He stood in the living room and gazed at the couch. He could almost imagine himself sleeping there, but why would he, if he were married to Holly? They had a fight, but he wasn't sure how he knew that. The stairs creaked, so he slipped into the kitchen where he spotted the basement door. Perfect, he thought and hurried inside just as Bill and Holly's mother entered the kitchen.

"What did the police say, Bill? Do they have any leads, any suspects? Anything?" She sat in a chair by the table. "I don't know how Holly is going to pull through this without him."

"I know." Bill gently touched her shoulder. "She's sleeping now, so let her sleep. We'll start over tomorrow."

"I have to work tomorrow. I can't take any more days off, but I'm going to request working part-time. This way, Holly won't be completely alone."

"I'll check in on her." Bill opened a cupboard and grabbed a glass, filling it with water. He took a long drink. What? No gin and tonic, Gary thought, but this time, he kept his mouth shut. "I won't leave her alone," Bill said.

"Neither will I," Gary whispered.

"It's late. I have to go." He dropped the glass into the sink and began to wash it. He dried it with a paper towel and returned it to its rightful place. "Will you be okay?" Holly's mother nodded. "Lock the doors and windows after I leave."

"Are we in danger?"

"No. The cops don't suspect foul play."

"Do you?" Holly's mother rose from her chair and crossed her arms over her chest. "Do you think that someone killed him?"

"I don't know what to think, but we can't allow ourselves to think like that." He kissed her on the cheek and then showed himself out. "Get some sleep."

"You too." She hurried behind him and locked the door the moment he closed it.

Gary decided the safest bet was to wait awhile for her to fall asleep. He bided his time with the events of the day. How strange they were, he thought, and still, no answers. There was nobody who could answer his questions. He was here, stuck in this reality, but this place was much better, safer than his home. But what about the other him? Would he be as fortunate? A knot turned in his stomach. He didn't want to know, and just as he started to doze, he realized that the house was quiet. Now was his chance. He opened the basement door and stepped into a dark kitchen, making his way up the stairs and to Holly's room.

"Holly?" He wavered over her as she lay on her back, looking like an angel. "Holly, I missed you." His lips brushed against hers, and he savored her scent. His heart broke as he remembered his loss, but she was here now. She was alive in this world. "Holly, I love you."

"Gary?" Holly opened her eyes and stared up into his face. "Gary?" She saw his scar and screamed.

The lights flashed on, and Holly's mother hurried inside. She wrapped her arms around Holly and tried to calm her down. Her daughter stuttered and stammered, but she hushed her like a baby girl. "It's all right, Holly." Her mother kissed Holly's forehead.

"He was here. He was here, but it wasn't him. It was him, but it wasn't." She burst into tears.

"Holly, he's gone. I'm sorry." She held Holly tighter in her arms. "He's gone," she whispered, and Holly cried harder. "I'm sorry, Holly. I'm so sorry." She cried with her. "Do you want me to stay in here tonight?" Holly shook her head. "Are you sure?"

"I'm okay, Mom. It was just a dream." Holly shuddered, but she shook it off. "It was just a dream."

"Okay. I'm right next door in the guest room, if you need me. Okay?"

"Okay, Mom."

"I love you, Holly."

"I love you too." Holly lay back down and watched her mother leave the room. The lights turned off, and the bedroom door closed. Her eyes darted around the walls, looking for shadows, looking for him, but maybe, it was a dream. If it was a dream, why did she still sense him? The thought of losing him broke her heart. She burst into tears, sobbing into the pillow, and Gary lay underneath the bed, listening to her cry and silently shedding his own tears.

When he was absolutely sure that Holly had fallen back asleep, he slowly rolled out from underneath the bed. He quietly stood up and took a cautious step toward her. He wanted to touch her face again. He wanted to kiss her, but instead his fingers reached for a strand of her hair. She was alive, and that was more than enough for him right now. He quickly left the room, and as the door closed behind him, she opened her eyes.

As he stood in the hallway, trying to figure out his next step, Gary looked up at the ceiling. He reached for the attic door and pulled it down, and as it creaked, he froze. He waited a beat and then moved the ladder down toward him. He climbed upward, not sure what to expect, and then pulled the ladder up and closed the door. This is where I will stay, close to her.

There was a small, dusty window facing out over the driveway. He glimpsed outside and then banged his head on a hanging light bulb. How many times did the other him do that? He spotted tons of boxes, all covered in dust and spider webs, and he shuddered. He hated spiders, but this would be a better hiding spot than the basement, which was too open with no exit. As he started to dig around in the attic, he found a rolled up sleeping bag and a bear-shaped pillow, which he bet belonged to Holly, and that was just fine with him. He made a spot on the floor behind some boxes, and curling up into a ball, he fell asleep.

It was late morning when he awoke. The house was still quiet, and he looked outside the window to see the driveway was empty. Holly's mother must have gone to work, which meant that just he and Holly were here. He didn't want to scare her again, but maybe, he could still sneak into her bedroom and grab some of the other Gary's clothes. If he couldn't, it didn't matter. He would figure something else out.

As he crept down from the attic, he thought he heard something. It was a strange noise but one that he recognized, and his stomach turned over. He lifted up the ladder and closed the attic door before tiptoeing over to Holly's room. The sound got louder, and as he nudged the bedroom door open, he realized that she was in the bathroom with the door closed. She was throwing up.

This would be his only chance, so he quickly moved inside. He opened the closet and grabbed a few shirts. Then, he opened the dresser drawers, grabbing everything else. He pushed the drawers shut and started to leave the room when he heard her voice.

"Hello? Is someone there?" She gagged once again, but now she was finished. "Mom?" Gary wanted to answer, but he forced himself out. She wasn't ready yet, and he would not hurt her again. "Gary?" He froze and then closed the bedroom door behind him. "Mom?" Holly stepped into the bedroom and looked around the room. "I thought I heard someone." She shook her head. "Holly, you're going crazy." She crawled into the bed and stared up at the ceiling. "He's dead, Holly. You saw what happened to him, and nobody will believe you. How could he have survived that," and with that horrible image inside her mind, she burst into tears.

Gary slid down the wall outside her room and listened to her cry. He knew her tears so well. He reached for the door but then thought better of it. Holding the clothes in his arms, he lowered his head, silently sharing her pain. She had said something, something strange. Did she know what happened to him and the other him? If she did, then she knew. The other him was never coming back.

After she had finally cried herself to sleep, he moved away and down the hall to the guest bathroom. He pulled a towel from the hall closet and then stepped inside. The hot water on his skin was welcoming, especially on his back, as he tried to wash away that other life. When he was all dry and dressed, he took his old clothing, found a black garbage bag, put the clothes into it, and dropped it down into the basement. He flipped open the pocket watch and stared at Holly's face. This was their chance, but now was not the time.

Two months later. Gary had fallen into a perfect routine. Holly's mother now worked eight a.m. to one p.m., and Bill visited in the evenings. There was plenty of time to move around the house, watch some television, eat, and take showers. There was also time to check in on Holly and sit outside her room, sharing the time with her and wishing she knew. It was the weekends that were the hardest, and most of the time, he was trapped in the attic. But he managed every now and then to sneak out and use the bathroom.

Holly had cried herself to sleep for a month and a half. She then stopped crying, and she stopped talking. The only time she did talk was to inquire about Gary. Did they find him? Are they still looking? Is he dead? Is he coming home?

Nobody had any answers, and neither did Gary. Holly was eating more, and she seemed different, sure of something. But what? What had she figured out? Did she know that he was there, and if she did, then why didn't she say anything?

"Holly?" Bill opened her bedroom door. "I've got dinner. Meatloaf, potatoes, and green beans." Gary's mouth watered as he pressed his ear against the attic floor to listen in. "There's plenty, so whatever you don't eat tonight, you can have in the morning." Gary smiled. "Holly?"

"Sure. Bring it in, Bill." She sat up in bed and gestured toward the chair nearby. "How's your wife doing?"

"She's good. How are you doing?" He took a seat beside the bed and gently handed her the tray. "Your mother said that you haven't been saying much."

"What do you want me to say?" Holly began to eat her dinner. "I want my husband back?" She paused as Bill cracked open a can of soda. "They won't find him."

"Yes, they will." He handed her the can of soda. "He's alive, Holly." She took a sip of the soda. "I know it," he said, but she didn't have the heart to tell him that he was wrong. "He's coming home, I promise." He watched her eat her dinner. "Hey, you remember your twenty-fifth birthday at that Mexican restaurant?" She slowly nodded. "Remember that they put that sombrero on your head, and you kept complaining about something scratching your hair." Holly giggled. "You finally took that sombrero off your head, and a cockroach fell to the floor." He laughed, and she laughed with him.

"You know, I'm trying to eat my dinner here." She laughed, and Bill chuckled. But then she grew serious. "I'm sorry, Bill."

"For what?"

"For choosing Gary, but we always had this connection. And…"

"Holly, it's okay. I know things got awkward afterward at the law firm where you interned."

"Temp. I was a temporary legal secretary, and Gary talked me into moving in with him. And then, he proposed, and we came here soon afterward. He even got you to come with us."

"And it was here in this town, where I met my wife. See? Everything worked out like it was supposed to."

"What if he isn't coming back?"

"He's coming back, Holly." Bill touched her hand but then pulled it away. "Whatever happened to him, it doesn't matter. You two are like soul mates, and he loves you a great deal. So, trust me. He's coming back."

"What if he's different?"

"Different?" He watched Holly glance up at the ceiling. "Have you seen him or heard from him?" She shook her head. "Is there anything that I should know?"

"I dug around through his dresser drawers," Holly said, "I found this." She reached under her pillow and pulled out a small stack of envelopes tied together. "He tried to hide them in the back of a drawer, but I found them. Bill, it's hate mail and death threats. They're dated before he disappeared." She handed them to Bill. "I think someone was trying to kill him, but... I don't think they did."

"I didn't know about these." Bill looked through the small stack in his hands. "But I'll take them to the police." He was quiet for a moment. "I think Gary's alive."

"I know," Holly whispered, and again, she glanced up at the ceiling. "Maybe, he is." Bill followed her gaze and now stared up at the ceiling. "I'm tired."

"Okay." He moved away from her bed. "I'll check in on you tomorrow night." He started to open the bedroom door. "You know, Holly, in this job, we do make enemies."

"I know, and sometimes, it's just better to hide the truth."

"Yeah." He glanced up at the ceiling. "Sometimes." He left the room.

Outside Holly's bedroom, Bill looked up at the attic door. He slowly moved toward it. He reached up for the door when he heard creaking along the stairs, and he knew it was Holly's mother. Should he tell her? Probably not. At least, not right now.

"Bill? Are you going up to the attic?" Gary froze at her words. "Need a hand?"

"No. I was just looking for a.... That bear-shaped pillow that Gary got her at a fair, but I can look tomorrow. It's late." He checked his watch. "I should go."

"Bill, what are you holding?" Holly's mother gestured toward the small stack of envelopes in his hands. "What's that?"

"Nothing. Just mail." He moved toward the stairs.

"Bill." He froze on a step at the tone of her voice. "You know, how I feel about liars, so I'm just going to ask once. Are you lying to me?"

"Look, it's nothing. Everything's fine." He moved down a step. "I have to go."

"Then, go." Holly's mother watched him leave, and then she turned toward the bedroom door. She opened it a little to see Holly still eating the rest of her dinner and decided not to bother her, but something was up. She wandered over to the attic door, but she didn't open it. Would Gary be such an idiot to hide out here while his sick wife needed him? "You'd better not be up there," she said. "You hear me? You'd better not be up there." She walked into her room and slammed the door closed.

Gary cursed under his breath. He was busted, but at least, he had two months to be near Holly. Now, it would either be Bill or Holly's mother who would catch him up here, and then what would he do? He was not the man that they were looking for. They would see that from the scar on his face, and then they would freak out. He had to leave, and since Holly's mother wasn't coming up here anytime soon, he would leave in the morning. But where would he go? His mind worked quickly, flashing back over all those photo albums that he went through. He grabbed a box nearby and dug through it until he found a blue envelope with an old, faded birthday card inside. On the envelope was a return address, the home address to a family that he never knew. That was where he would go next.

It was just before one in the afternoon. The attic door opened. Footsteps echoed up the ladder. A head banged into a hanging light bulb. A curse echoed throughout the cramped space, and boxes were pushed aside. A flattened sleeping bag and a crushed bear-shaped pillow were found on the floor.

"Gary." Bill knelt down and picked up the bear-shaped pillow. "Holly was right. You were up here, but why didn't you tell us?"

"Bill?" Holly's mother stood at the bottom of the ladder. "What are you doing up there?"

"Looking for this," he said quickly, holding the bear-shaped pillow in his arms. "I'm coming down."

"Was he up there?" She watched Bill push the ladder up and close the attic door. "Don't lie to me." She read the expression on his face and knew. "Oh my God. He was. He was up there. Why? Why would he do that to her, to my Holly? Why?"

"Keep your voice down," Bill hissed as he led her away from where they were standing. "Is she asleep?"

"She's in and out." Holly's mother crossed her arms over her chest. "Bill, why would he do this to her?"

"Maybe to protect her?"

"From what? What is going on, and don't tell me those letters you had was just mail. Tell me the truth for once."

"Fine." He led her down the stairs. "The police have a suspect in custody." Her face brightened. "He was the one sending Gary hate mail and death threats."

"Death threats? Bill, I asked you if we were in danger, and you said no."

"I didn't know until last night." He could tell she wanted to slap him across the face, so he told her the rest. "When the police arrested him this morning, he was soaked in blood, someone else's blood." Her hand fluttered up over her mouth. "That's why I came over. I was hoping that he was still here, but he must've heard us talking. And he must've run."

"Bill, you don't think that he was murdered, do you?"

"I don't know. The police are running DNA now." He stared up at the ceiling. "Gary put this guy away for murder, and he got out on probation." He looked at Holly's mother. "He was trying to protect Holly."

"Not by lying to her." Holly's mother grabbed the bear-shaped pillow out of Bill's hand and moved back toward Holly's bedroom.

"Don't tell Holly."

"She deserves to know, Bill."

"You remember what the doctor said. She can't lose the baby." He turned to see her standing outside the bedroom door. "She nearly lost her. Do you really want her to miscarry?"

"No," Holly's mother said. "I don't."

"Then, leave her alone. At least, for now." She slowly followed him down the stairs. "I'll work with the police and find out what they know."

"Okay," Holly's mother said. "Maybe, he's still alive."

"Maybe," Bill responded. "Let's hope so."

"He's alive," Holly whispered as she leaned against her bedroom door. "It wasn't Gary. He was here, but he wasn't here." She wiped her tears away. "He was struck by lightning, and he was gone. And he's not coming back." She wrapped her arms around her belly. "Who was in my attic? Was it that man with a scar, and why did he look like Gary?" She got back into bed. "Gary, was that you?"

One month later. A soft mist settled over brown earth. Flowers bit into the gray. A gentle breeze rustled past American flags. Shadows fell over stone, and benches waited for those to forget time, to sit for a while, and to remember those now gone.

    Gary sat on one of those benches in front of his father's grave. Well, the other Gary's father, but he sounded like a great man from what he had read. This man had fought in Vietnam, came home and started a family, his family, but a family that he would never know.

"Gary?" He looked up to see a young woman holding a black umbrella over her head. She had a newspaper tucked under one arm and flowers in her other hand. "I'm sorry, but you look just like a friend of mine."

"I get that a lot." Gary stared at her. "Are you family?" He gestured toward his father's grave.

"No. Just a close friend." She continued to stare at him. "You look like him. Gary. Well, except for the scar." Gary gingerly touched the jagged line across his face. "I'm sorry."

"Don't be." He watched her place the flowers against his father's grave.

"Everybody has a doppelganger."

"I guess so." She took a step away from the grave and then turned toward him. "I'm Barbara."

"Nice to meet you."

"Same here." She sat down at the edge of the stone bench. "What's your name?" He didn't answer her. How could he? She was already suspicious. "Can you at least tell me how you got that scar?"

"Bar fight."

Gary wished his foster father was six feet down. He wasn't. This man went to war for his country, but his foster father went to war with himself. He came home late, drunk, and used Gary as a punching bag. His foster father almost killed him once, and that was where the scar really came from. And that was the last time that he would ever touch Gary, and that was the first time that Gary had to disappear. "I'm not him," Gary said.

"I know, but you look just like him." She stared at him. "He's been missing for three months now." She pulled the newspaper out from under her arm. "The police had a suspect, but they were wrong."

"The Waken Herald?" He stared at the newspaper. "You get that newspaper all the way up here?"

"My friend, Eric sends these to me," she answered him.

"Can I see it?" She hesitated and then handed the newspaper to him. "Thank you." He stared at the front page. "Prime Suspect Guilty in Death of Witness Denies Murdering Prominent Lawyer," he read.

"Gary," she said.

Barbara was right. The front-page article was all about him. Well, the other him. Apparently, Gary had led the prosecution against this man, and with a witness's testimony, the man was locked up in prison for five years. Then, he made probation, and he wrote the hate mail and death threats that Holly had found. But he was too late in trying to kill Gary, but he succeeded in killing the witness. If the police hadn't caught him, Gary wondered if he would have come looking for him. If he had, that man would have regretted that decision, but luckily for him, he was going back to prison. And he was never coming out.

"I have to go." She stood up and held out her hand, waiting for the newspaper. "It was nice meeting you?"

"It was nice meeting you too." He handed her the newspaper, knowing that she still wanted his name. "Take care."

She took the newspaper back and moved away, but then she stopped to look at him once more. "If you're not him, then why are you sitting here? Why are you staring at Gary's father's grave?" She waited for an answer, then shook her head and walked away.

Gary turned toward the grave and stared at it. She knew who he was, but she didn't freak out like Holly did. "Sorry, Dad, but I'm not him. I'm not your Gary." He stood up from the bench. "Your Gary was no saint either."

During his time at Holly's house, he hung out in the den. First, he was amused by the cluttered office. Then, he tried accessing Gary's computer, and of course, the password was Holly. There wasn't much use for that computer afterward except to look at past and present cases. The Randall case was a big case, one that could've made Gary's career. Apparently, a local man was scamming thousands of dollars from local nursing homes, and on top of that, he had his mistress murdered. Gary put him away just like the man who wanted to kill him, and that was that for the computer.

In the den, he also discovered a hidden panel in the closet, and inside that space was eighteen hundred dollars in cash and a silver handgun. Why, Gary thought. Was his other self going to buy someone off or kill them? It didn't matter. He was gone, and this Gary was left. And he could use that money. He could also use that gun.

"I wish I knew you." He touched the smooth stone surface. "I've seen Mom so many times, but she hasn't seen me. I should say good-bye to her before I leave. Maybe, she would understand." His hand rested on the tombstone. "Would you have believed me?" A moment of silence passed. "No, I don't think you or she would, but I want to know. Why did you get rid of me?" He walked away, leaving the cemetery behind.

The motel where he resided was only a few miles away from his would-be parents' house. He got a rental car and passed through the neighborhood several times. Sometimes, he parked outside and stared at his would-be family through their windows. He had siblings, siblings that now threw strange glances his way. He ducked down to avoid their gazes. Still, it felt good being close to home. Well, the other Gary's home.

It was getting dark outside. His stomach roared, reminding him that he had forgot lunch again. He should call the house, his mother, but he checked his pocket watch first. He stared down at Holly's face for a moment and finally looked at the time. His family was probably eating dinner now and wouldn't answer the phone anyway. He would get dinner and then make the call, but he felt his knees go weak at that thought. He had stayed here for too long, and he wanted to go back. He needed to go back for Holly. He couldn't leave her behind.

An hour later, he sat on the bed, which squeaked beneath him. He cradled the phone in his hands. He was sweating, and his heart was racing. There were so many times when he saw his mother, but he couldn't talk to her. What if she thought that he was the other Gary? What if she realized that he wasn't? What if she thought that he had killed her son, and in a way, he did. He could feel the other Gary's blood on his hands, and he knew that their Gary was dead.

"Hello?"

Gary slammed the phone down and dropped it onto the bed. "It's just a phone call, Gary," he said. "Just call her. Hear her voice one last time, but this time, she will be speaking to you. And then you go home. You go home to Holly." He paced around the room but then paused in front of a full-length mirror. He stared at his scar and traced its jagged line with his finger. "What? What are you looking at," Gary yelled at himself. "Damn you for doing this to me. If there was no scar, I could be him. I would be him. He was me, after all, and I could be him!"

He slammed his fist into the mirror. Shards spilled everywhere, and blood ran down his hand. "You ruined my life, Dad. You made me this person." He glared at the fragments left in the mirror, which split him into several images of himself. "I went to prison because I almost killed you, and it was there that I met Dell. And everything went to hell afterward until I met her." He struck the mirror again, wincing in pain. "It's not fair," he cried. "She's alive, and I can't have her! But I will."

There was a knock on his motel door. Who would be knocking at this hour? Maybe, one of his neighbors thought he was in trouble or wanted to complain about the noise. It didn't matter. Maybe, they would just go away. Instead, another knock came, louder this time. "What?" Gary threw open the door. "Mom?"

She flinched at that word. "No. Um.... Can I come in?" His mother, the other Gary's mother stood outside his door. Her eyes were red, probably from crying, but was she crying about him? "Can I come in?" She asked again, and Gary gestured for her to go inside. "Thank you." She looked down at his hand and then over at the mirror. "You hurt your hand."

"It's fine."

"No, it's not." She stood a short distance away from him. Part of her wanted to run, but she forced herself to look at him. And she looked at his hand again. "You have any band-aids?"

"Maybe." He moved toward the bathroom. "Let me check." Luckily, the former tenant had left peroxide and band-aids in the medicine cabinet. Gary brought them out, half expecting his mother to be gone, but she was still there, watching him like a hawk. "Here." He laid the stuff out on a wooden table and sat down in a chair nearby.

"I was at the cemetery today, and I saw you talking to Barbara." She pulled another chair toward him and sat down. "I heard what you said." He looked away. "You're him, but you're not." She reached for his injured hand, and he met her gaze. "You have my father's eyes. My Gary did too." She began to pull little shards out of his hand. "If not for that scar, you would look just like him."

"I know," Gary whispered.

"How did you get that scar?"

"My foster father." He hissed as she poured a peroxide over his hand. "I almost killed him." She froze for a moment and then resumed pulling band-aids out of the box. "I went to jail for a while, and then I met a bad man there. Everything went to hell afterward."

"I'm sorry," his mother said.

"Don't be." He pulled his hand away and looked it over. "Thank you."

"I have to know." She sat back in her chair. "Is my son coming back?" He shook his head, and tears ran down her face. "I see. Is he dead?"

"If that bad man found him, then yes. He's dead." Those words hurt him more than he thought they would. "I'm sorry."

"What's his name?"

"Who?"

"The bad man."

"Dell."

"Dell," she repeated. "You were friends with him?"

"He tried to kill me. He nearly did before…"

"Before?"

"I came here."

"How? How did you get here?"

"I was struck by lightning." He watched her reaction, shocked that she believed him. "You believe me?" He watched her nod. "Your son was struck by lightning too, and we switched places. And I'm stuck here." She was quiet for a moment, letting his words sink in. "I'm sorry. I really am, but I can't go back. I don't know how." He moved away from her. "I should leave." He grabbed a black duffel bag off the floor. "I'm sorry," he said.

"Stop apologizing. My children wanted to call the police." He turned toward her. "They kept telling me that someone was spying on us, watching our house, staring through the windows."

"I was curious."

"I knew something was wrong, but I'm not completely wrong." She stared at him. "I understand why you were reluctant to come to me, but calling and hanging up?"

"I'm sorry."

"Don't apologize. I knew you were him when I saw you, but I was afraid too." She stood up from her seat and approached him. She cautiously touched his face, his scar. "You are my son."

"No, I'm not," Gary said. "I told you what I did."

"Look at your face." He flinched, slowly turning toward the broken mirror nearby. "That monster did this to you, so I don't care about that. And I don't want you to leave."

"I have to, Mom." She flinched again.

"And go where?" She took his hands in hers. "Please. Please, don't leave. I have so many questions, and I know you do too. I won't tell my children about you, but please, don't leave. Not yet." He looked into her eyes, and again, he could feel his heart break. "Please, stay here just for a little while longer. With me."

"What about Holly?"

"Holly? You know who she is?"

"Of course, I do." He squeezed his mother's hands. "In my reality, she saved me from Dell." Now, he started to cry. "But she was dying, and I lost her. And I came here, and she's here. And she's alive, and I love her. I love her so much."

"I always thought that my Gary and Holly were meant to be. I guess I was right, and he loved her. He loved her as much as you do." She pulled her hands away. "I should call her. See how she is, and I can give you updates on how she's doing."

"You can't tell her."

"I know, Gary." They both flinched when she said his name, but she called him, Gary. "I know my son when I look at him, and you are my son." He dropped the duffel bag to the floor. "You'll stay?"

"I'll stay." He half expected her to hug him, but she was still nervous. He couldn't blame her for that. "I do have questions."

"So do I. How about breakfast tomorrow? I'll meet you here at ten a.m.?" He nodded, and she moved toward the door. "I'll see you in the morning, and I'll call Holly."

"I'll see you in the morning." He watched her leave and whispered, "Mom."

Two months later. During the first month, they barely left the motel. Gary's mother brought food in, and they talked. There were so many questions on both sides, and both of them did their best to answer the questions. Then, they just spent time together, and toward the end of the first month, his mother started to stay over every other night to keep him company. During the second month, they ventured out into town, but she wouldn't go to her favorite places. Her Gary was still missing, and she led her children to believe that she was seeing another man. She just didn't tell them that the man was their brother from an alternate reality.

"I have a question," she said as they left a movie theater one night. "How did you know what your real name was, if you were in foster care?"

"That's a funny story." He got into her car. "You remember that bad man, Dell?"

"Unfortunately. I try not to think of him, but I find myself wondering if he killed my son." She didn't start the ignition but sat back in the darkness. "He's dead, isn't he?" Gary nodded. "I hope that bastard, Dell rots in hell."

"People like him usually do."

"So, what's your funny story?"

"Well, I was turning thirty-two, and Dell surprised me with an early birthday gift. It was my original birth certificate with my real name, Gary Javin."

"What was your name before that?"

"I had so many." Gary laughed, but she didn't. "When I saw my name, that's who I became, Gary Javin. It didn't matter who I was before that."

"Was I listed on the birth certificate?"

"Yes, but no father's name." He looked at her. "He never came home from war."

"I was always afraid of that," she said. "It's my fault what happened to you."

"Mom…"

"No. At that time, I didn't think I could raise a child, and if he never came home, then I was going to give you away, hoping that you found a better home. Instead, I destroyed your life." She touched his face, rubbing a finger against his scar. "This is my fault."

"Mom, don't." He grabbed her hand and held it against his chest. "All the wrong that I did was my doing not yours, and I told you that Holly saved me. If there wasn't any good in me that I got from you, then she wouldn't have. I probably would have killed her and put her out of her misery."

"Don't say that."

"You don't know Dell."

"No, but I know you." She pressed her hand against his chest. "You have a good heart, and you got a second chance."

"But you lost your Gary. She pulled her hand away. "He should be here. Not me."

"It wasn't your doing." She wiped her tears away. "My kids are asking about you, but I can't tell them."

"I know. Have you checked in on Holly?"

"Not recently, but I'll do it tomorrow before I come over." She started the ignition but then looked over at him. Lately, it felt like she wanted to tell him something, but for whatever reason, she wasn't. "I can't believe it's been five months since he's been gone." She looked away, and he remained quiet. "I'll drop you off, and then I have to go home tonight." He nodded and stayed quiet all the way to the motel.

"Good-night." He exited the car and watched her drive away. "I'm sorry," he whispered. "I really am."

The loud knock at his motel door came at 9 a.m. He nearly jumped out of bed. His hand reached under the pillow and closed over the silver handgun. He thought about it and then left it where it was. Then, another knock came. He hurried over to the door and reached for the doorknob. If it were the police, they would have broken the door down by now. And Dell? He wasn't hunting him in this reality, so he relaxed and opened the door.

"Gary, it's Holly." His mother hurried past him. "She was rushed back to the hospital this morning."

"What? What happened?"

"I don't know. Her mother was vague on the phone, and she was in a hurry. She didn't tell me anything except her daughter left in an ambulance to the hospital."

"I have to go." He once again grabbed the black duffel bag off the floor.

"I know. You want me to book you a flight?"

"No, I can take the rental." He looked at her and smiled. "Thank you."

"Gary, will you come back?" He paused in front of the dresser and glanced at her. "I lost my son. I don't want to lose you too."

He knew that she was waiting for an answer, but what could he say? Was he coming back? He didn't know. He had to go back to Waken, and under normal circumstances, he would say that he was coming back. But his life and this situation were far from normal, and after returning to Waken, all bets were off. "I'll come back," he said, but she didn't believe him. "I'll try to come back. I should get dressed."

"I'll wait." She sat in a chair by the table.

Twenty minutes later, he was ready to go. His mother followed him over to his car. He hugged her, and she started to cry. He hated that he always made her cry, but some of those tears were now of happiness. She hugged him tightly, afraid to let go. "I'll try to come back," he said.

"If you do…" She finally released her hold on him. "I'll tell my family about you."

"They won't understand."

"They can try." She touched his face. "Come back. Soon."

"I love you, Mom." She did not flinch when he said that.

He got into his car and closed the driver-side door. He stared at her for a long time and then finally started the ignition. He pulled out of the parking lot and headed for the main road. He glanced up at the rearview mirror to see his mother waving at him. "Good-bye," and he drove away into the distance ahead.

As he reached his last toll, he glanced up at the sky. Not a cloud was to be seen. A cool breeze rustled through the open window. Would he be here to see the year end? Would he be with her? "Holly." He failed to see the surveillance camera overhead. "Please, be okay." He leaned out the window and handed the tollbooth attendant cash. He waited for his change and drove away. "Please, be okay," he whispered.

Once back in Waken, Gary tried to determine the next course of action. Holly wasn't home, and neither was her mother. It was easy to assume that they were still at the hospital, but what about Bill? Seeing his Jeep Liberty was still parked in front of his law office, Gary knew what he would have to do, but was it the right thing to do?

Six p.m. Bill got into his car and started the ignition. He checked his cell phone, which was quiet, and dropped it into the cup holder. He looked over his shoulder and checked the rearview mirror. He was all set to move the gear from park to drive when he sensed someone behind him. He looked in the rearview mirror again. "Gary," he gasped.

"Eyes forward, Bill. I don't want you looking at my face."

"Gary." Bill turned toward him.

"No! Eyes forward." Bill slowly turned back around toward the steering wheel. "I'm sorry, but you can't look at my face."

"Why?"

"Because you won't understand."

"Gary, we've known each other for a long time now. I can understand anything. Just tell me. Why are you hiding? What happened to you?"

"You won't understand." Gary remained behind the driver's seat. "Tell me about Holly."

"What about her?"

"Why is she back in the hospital?"

"You should see for yourself."

"That's not an answer, Bill."

"I'm not giving you an answer, Gary. How could you do this to me, to her? What the hell is wrong with you?" Bill cut the ignition. "You're breaking her heart, and you know how that makes me feel."

"You never told her, did you?"

"I promised you that I wouldn't, Gary."

"I heard that sombrero story, and I figured it out. You love her."

"You knew that before you even proposed to her." Bill tore off his seatbelt. "What is this?" He turned toward him, and Gary moved back into the darkness to hide his face. "What is this!"

"This was a mistake." Gary exited the car. "Don't follow me."

"Fuck you." Bill leaped out of his car after him. "Fuck you, Gary!" He grabbed him and spun him around, and he saw his face. "You're not Gary," he gasped. "You can't be."

"I am." Gary felt sad at Bill's reaction, but he warned him. And like with the Bill in his world, he always did what he wanted to do. "I warned you."

"What is this?" Bill demanded. "What's going on? What's wrong with your face?"

"I'm from an alternate reality, Bill."

"You're crazy."

"Then, tell me another explanation." Bill fell quiet. "You can't because you don't understand, and this…" He pointed at his scar. "This is exactly why I've been hiding."

"Who are you?"

"I'm Gary. Just not your Gary."

"What do you want?" Bill leaned against his car. His face mingled with fear and concern. "What do you want with Holly?"

"I love her."

"You don't know her."

"Yes, I do, but she died in my reality."

"So, you're going to take my Holly instead?" Gary stared at him. "She doesn't know you, and you probably scared the hell out of her, didn't you? Staying at her house? Spying on her?" Now, Bill was enraged. "You can't have her. I won't let you." He was inches away from Gary. "You can't have her," he snarled.

"I want her to decide that." Gary took a step back. "You said that we were like soul mates. I fell in love with her in my reality, and…"

"And you lost her."

"And your Gary fell in love with her in this reality. What does that tell you, Bill?" Now, Bill took a step back. "We're meant to be. I love her, and she loves me."

"She doesn't love you. She loves Gary."

"I am Gary." They stared at each other for a moment. "Look, I didn't want this to go this way. I'm sorry. I thought staying away from her would protect her from the truth, but the truth is that I need her. And she needs me."

"Give her time," Bill said. "She needs time, Gary." He flinched as he said that.

"Just answer one question for me." Bill nodded. "Is she dying?"

"No. Why would you ask me that?" He realized how this Gary lost his Holly. "I'm sorry."

"I just needed to know." Gary walked away.

"Gary?" He turned toward Bill. "What was I in your reality?"

"A famous lawyer. You even had your own billboard sign." He moved away. "You were a prick, though," he said. "I like who you are in this reality." Gary crossed the street and disappeared into the parking lot.

"Gary." Bill scratched the back of his head. "What happened to my friend?" But deep down, he knew. His friend was never coming back. "What do I tell Holly and her baby girl?"

Gary got into the rental car. He looked up at the law firm and saw that Bill was still standing outside his vehicle. He was probably in shock, and Gary couldn't blame him. Bill knew the truth now that his friend was never coming back, but what was Bill going to tell Holly? What was Gary going to tell her when she came home? Would she love him like she did her Gary? He hoped so.

Sitting in his car felt like forever, but only ten minutes flashed across the car radio. There was only one place left to go. Bill knew the truth now, and so would Holly. He would wait at the house for them to come home. Then, if she asked him to leave, he would and never come back, but if she asked him to stay, he would stay. He revved up the engine and headed for Holly's house, hoping that she would ask him to stay. "Please, Holly," he thought.

"Please, give me a chance."

As Gary pulled up across from Holly's house, he could've sworn that he saw a flash of light in the living room. The house fell back into darkness, and he exited the car. Maybe, he was seeing things, but there it was again. It was a flashlight swinging back and forth, and now it was in the dining room. Someone was in the house, and it wasn't Holly or her mother. It was someone else, and Gary would be damned if he would let anyone hurt Holly or her mother.

He snuck around back like he had done before and grabbed a baseball bat. He tested the slider door and again found it unlocked. He walked into the house with the baseball bat in hand and the silver handgun tucked into the back of his pants under his shirt. He crept forward in the darkness, but there was no more flashlight beam. Whoever was here knew that he had entered the house, and he took a step forward. He made it to the stairs when a shadow rose up behind him, picked up a lamp off a wooden table and smashed it against his head.

Darkness. Pain. A bright light flashed overhead. It was the dining room light, and a face leaned over his. A sharp finger poked at his scar, drawing blood, and he struggled to recognize the man that hovered above him. It was him. Another Gary.

"Wakey. Wakey," he said. "Time to wake up, beautiful." His other self took a step back, almost admiring him. "If it wasn't for that scar, you would be beautiful. What? Cat got your tongue?"

Gary realized that he was tied to the dining room table. He was held in a T shape with his arms stretched outward on both sides and his legs bound together. His mouth wasn't taped shut, which meant that his other self wanted answers, but one thing was clear. Seeing the knives laid out nearby, he knew that he was dead. If only he could reach for his gun.

"You probably know already what I intend to do." He lifted up a knife and tested its sharpness by pushing his finger against it, drawing blood. "Who would have thunk that Waken wasn't a city but a town, a town ripe for me?"

"Let me guess," Gary said. "You're my insane half?"

"Careful." He waved the knife at him. "You know, never in my wildest imaginations have I ever thought of killing myself, which should be interesting." He walked over to Gary with the knife in his hand. "When I was eight, I ran away from that foster care shit. I lived on the streets like an animal, unwanted and cold, and then I met a man, a man, who is responsible for the well-adjusted person that I became today."

"Well-adjusted, my ass." Gary laughed. "You're worse than Dell."

"Dell? That pussy and his bitch Marc couldn't hold a candle to me, and it was a pleasure killing them both."

"You killed them?"

"Of course, I did." He ran a black gloved hand through Gary's hair, pulling some strands out. "I killed Bill Henders too, but surprise, surprise. He's alive and well in this reality. Well, not for long." He tapped the side of the knife against Gary's face. "And then there's Holly." He held Gary's gaze. "Oh, I saw that look in your eyes. I'll tell you this." He stepped an inch back. "I almost felt bad killing her."

"Do not fucking touch her," Gary yelled at him.

"Well, aren't we testy?" Gary tried to break free and realized that the rope around his left wrist was loose. If he could distract his other self, maybe he could break free. "How long have you been here?"

"How long have you been here?"

"You didn't answer my question." He plunged his knife deep into Gary's right calf, but Gary held back his scream. "Well, I guess you are me, so I'll answer your question." He ripped his knife out, ignoring the tear running down Gary's face. "Almost six months. It was like the fucking Twilight Zone, but then I realized something."

"What?" Gary turned his left wrist around and around, and as he did, the rope loosened.

"I could start over." He smiled to himself. "My city was my reign of terror, so why not do the same here to this town?" He leaned on top of Gary. "I kept myself busy killing beautiful women. I also did some research, and then I saw a copy of the Waken Herald. I was on the front page. 'Lawyer goes missing.' Can you believe that shit? I'm a lawyer in this reality? What a fucking waste. What did that guy have that we didn't?"

"A family." Gary's left hand was now free, and he punched his other self in the face, knocking him off the table. He went to work freeing his right hand, but his other self was quick, jumping back onto the table and landing on him. "Get off!"

"No." He plunged his knife into Gary's stomach, and Gary screamed. "There we go. Was that so hard to do, Gary? Look, this has been fun and everything, but I'm bored." He ripped out the knife, spilling blood everywhere. "I'll take care of Holly and Bill and Dell, if that piece of shit is still alive. I'll take care of all of them, but you… You'll be dead." He raised the knife over Gary's heart, and as his blade plunged down into Gary's chest, a gunshot went off.

His other self turned around to face someone. Another gunshot rang through the air, but his other self still didn't scream. He just looked at Gary and then fell backward onto the floor, still holding the knife in his hand. He gurgled and spat, trying to say something, but instead, he choked on his blood. Then, he was dead.

"Who are you?" Gary was losing consciousness fast. "Who are you!"

"Detective Green," and those words sent Gary into oblivion.

## CHAPTER FIVE

"Hey, what did your son bring you for lunch today?"

Detective Green leaned back in his chair, a manila folder resting on his lap. A picture of Gary Javin tried to escape, falling to the floor, but he grabbed hold of it quickly. He lifted the picture up, staring at Gary Javin's face. Then, he looked over at the lunch his son brought him. His son was on a mission lately for his father to eat healthy because he was diagnosed with high blood pressure. He knew his son was only looking out for him, but he still wanted his steak and bacon and egg sandwiches. "Egg whites on a roll." He dug through a paper brown bag. "A low-fat blueberry muffin and orange juice." He took the juice out and drank it. He pushed the rest of it away. "Eric means well, but even for dinner, he's now pushing me toward veggie burgers and salad." His partner, Harold laughed. "I'm glad he got his own apartment. Now, I have to change the locks at my house."

"Like you said, he means well." Harold sat at the edge of his desk and reached into the bag and grabbed the muffin. "You mind?"

"No. Take it. I'm not eating that."

"So, I guess we'll be stopping at a fast-food chain then?"

"Something like that. Any leads on your case?"

"No." Harold clapped his hands together, knocking the crumbs to the floor. He then scratched at his balding head. "Sick bastard. For the last few months or so, he's carved his way through this town, killing a lot of women." He glanced over at the manila folder. "What about your case? Any leads?"

"None," Detective Green said.

"I don't get it. The night that prominent lawyer goes missing, we have a wacko at the hospital, who threw himself out the window and disappeared. Then, we have another guy with a scar on his face pulling a Houdini act days later from the same hospital, and around this time, we have a serial killer, who just popped into town. I mean… Did I miss something, or what the hell is going on?" Still holding half a muffin in his hand, he crossed his arms over his chest.  "Oh, and the guy with the scar recently showed up on a surveillance camera coming back to Waken."

"What?" Detective Green sat up in his chair. "You couldn't have told me that sooner?"

"Relax. He came back, but he's not him. He's not your guy, even if the staff at the hospital swore up and down that he looked just like him except for the scar." Harold looked over at the picture of Gary Javin. He watched Detective Green take his pen and draw a jagged line from under Gary's right eye down toward his chin. "I mean it could be him, but where the hell did that scar come from? Anyway, I need to focus on this serial killer before the feds get involved."

"What about the last crime scene? Any DNA to chase down?"

"Maybe. The last victim did have DNA under her fingernails, and that's what I'm waiting on, for the lab to get back to me." Harold bit into the muffin, dropping more crumbs to the floor. He clapped his hands together and then wiped them on his lap. "Go find your guy." He watched Detective Green nod and move away from his desk. "But it can't be Gary Javin. He's probably dead and buried somewhere." Just then, a lab technician walked over to him with another manila folder. "It's about time." He took the folder and opened it. "Well, hello, Marc."

Six p.m. There was no telling when the guy with the scar would show up, but Doctor Wong had informed him of how he reacted to seeing Holly Javin in the hospital. And the only way to get to her was through Bill Henders, and he was right. Someone was in the back of Bill's car, talking to him, but Detective Green remained in his vehicle, watching the conversation spill outside of Bill's car. What were they arguing about? Holly? He was waiting for these two men to come to blows, but then the man with the scar crossed the street, heading in his direction.

Detective Green ducked down as he walked past the car. Apparently, he had parked in the row behind him. The headlights flashed on, but he remained where he was, sitting behind the steering wheel. What was he doing? Ten minutes later, he drove off and headed toward the Javin house. The detective followed.

A few minutes later after he had broken into the house, Detective Green made his move, exiting his vehicle and drawing his gun. He moved around back, opened the glass slider door, and walked inside. The only light on in the house was from the dining room, and he could hear two voices coming from that direction. They sounded identical, but two different men were talking. He edged closer. Nearing the stairs, he spied a broken lamp on the floor. He stepped over the porcelain shards and moved in closer. Then, he heard a scream. He moved faster, ready to fire, and as the knife raised in the air plunged downward, he fired. The man on the table turned toward him; it was Gary Javin. Detective Green fired again and watched that Gary Javin fall back onto the floor.

"Who are you?" the man on the table yelled.

"Detective Green." He watched the man pass out. He edged closer and took his pulse. Relieved that he was still alive, he pulled out his cell phone and punched in a number. "Bill? Yeah, it's Detective Green. Meet me at the Javin House. Now." He checked the pulse of the man on the floor. He was dead.

Detective Green lifted the dead man up into his arms, dragging him outside and placed him by the driveway. He took a step away when something struck the ground. Lightning. He spun around to see the dead Gary Javin lift up into the air and disappear.

"Shit," he said.

## CHAPTER SIX

Sunlight streamed in through a bedroom window. A cool breeze rustled through the room. Something metallic clinked against the brass headboard, and eyes opened to picture frames of a family he never knew. Another clink, a handcuff dangled against skin, and the bedroom door opened.

"Morning." Detective Green walked into the room. "Gary." The man just stared at him. "How are you feeling?"

"Sore." Gary struggled to sit up in the bed, flinching at the pain from his stab wounds. He stared at his right hand, which was handcuffed to the brass headboard. "Is that really necessary?"

"Yes." Detective Green moved closer and lifted up Gary's shirt, looking at his wounds. "They're healing nicely. The doctor did good work."

"Who patched me up?"

"Doctor Wong."

"What? Her? Why am I not in the hospital or jail?"

"She and I came to an understanding, so you're here in my house." He moved away. "Are you hungry? I made eggs."

"Am I your prisoner?"

He stood by the bedroom door. "Gary, I can't let you leave. You have to stay here. Now, do you want me to get you some eggs?"

"How do you know who I am?" He stared at the detective.

"Can I trust you?" The detective took a step toward him. "Or are you going to run?"

"I'm in no condition to run."

"Good, which makes it easier."

"For what?"

"Keeping you here."

"So, I am your prisoner. Detective?"

"Detective Green. Brian Green." He unhandcuffed Gary from the bed and then withdrew his gun. "Come on. Let's eat some breakfast." He gestured for Gary to move out of the bed.

Gary struggled to sit up. He was still sore and stitched up. "That's not necessary." He gestured toward the gun. "You saved my life, so I'll stay." He held out his hand toward the detective, who took it and pulled him to his feet. "Do I know you? Did the other Gary know you?"

"So, I guess no breakfast. Straight to the talking."

"Fine. Eggs first." Gary smiled. "But why do we need to talk? You don't know what's going on."

"Yes, I do."

Gary's smiled vanished.

"Let's eat first." Detective Green holstered his gun and left the room.

A little while later, Gary was in Detective Green's den. He watched the detective close the door and move over to a small bar, pulling out two shot glasses, and filling them with whiskey. It was a little too early in the morning to drink, but he could feel the tension already in the room. Then, he noticed a manuscript on the detective's desk. The detective handed him a shot glass, and even if it was too early for a drink, Gary still downed the liquid, savoring its taste.

"This your novel?" The detective nodded. "Is it finished?" The detective shook his head while downing his shot. Gary moved over to a glass bookcase. "May I?"

"Go ahead." The detective fell into his comfy, leather chair.

Gary opened the bookcase, gently swinging the glass doors away from him. On the top shelf were photographs of the detective and some girl. High School, maybe. On the shelf below were historical documents, all about Waken. On that same shelf was a framed newspaper article, and it was that one, which caught Gary's attention. It was the Waken Herald dated 1815, showing nothing but devastation. Its headline screamed: Town of Waken Wiped Out in Freak Storm.

"1815!"

"1815." The detective repeated. "I can't find anything before then. Everything was wiped out. Waken began again with that article, and we both know what happened. Don't we?" He watched Gary turned toward him, meeting his gaze. "Beware the storm, Gary. Beware the storm." He stared down at his empty shot glass.

"Are you…" Gary looked back at the bookcase and then down on the floor, and beside it was a football helmet. The helmet was red and gold, and there was a deep, scorch mark on top of it. Gary fell to his knees, his hands shaking as he touched the scorch mark. "Was this struck by…"

"Lightning," the detective said. He watched the color drain from Gary's face. He moved away from the chair and poured himself another drink. He downed it and was tempted to take another drink. Instead, he flipped the shot glass upside down and left it on the counter. "It's been thirty years, Gary. Thirty years, and I hoped, no, I prayed that what happened to me would never happen again to anyone." He turned toward Gary, who flinched at his stare. "It happened to you. You are from an alternate reality."

"Just like you." Gary slowly moved toward him. "You don't belong here." Gary watched the detective sit back down in his chair. "But you can't go back." Gary sat in a chair next to him. "There is no going back. Right?"

Detective Green stared at Gary for a long moment and then looked over at the football helmet. "I loved my life. I was the quarterback of Waken's high school football team. I was all set for college. One last game, and then I would graduate. And it was the fourth quarter with less than three minutes to go. We were winning. We were always winning, and scouts in the audience were watching me. I could've gone pro." He fell quiet, and Gary waited. "We were going to win, and then, it was over. It was all over, and I woke up in the hospital days later, dazed and confused. Nobody would give me any answers, but there were so many questions, especially why was I dressed as a football player and found lying in the middle of the high school field?" Again, he fell quiet, and again, Gary waited. "It took a long time to piece things together, but I kept my helmet. And I realized that I was struck by lightning, and there was no storm that night. No storm, but somehow, I switched places with another self. And no, I couldn't go back." He sighed and looked away. "My parents thought that I had gone crazy. Maybe, I was on drugs, but no drugs were found in my system. And apparently, my other self was not a jock and actually failing high school. It took a long time to adapt to his life, but I did it. And I didn't have a scar like you, so I understand why you went into hiding. But I'm glad that you came back."

"Why?" Gary watched the detective point over at the newspaper article. "I don't understand."

"As a cop, I had access to research whatever I wanted to research, so I researched this town. Like I said before, there is not a single record of Waken before 1815. Something went terribly wrong, and that storm came and wiped everything, everyone out. And that storm never returned again. Not until it came for me, but after that, nothing. Waken wasn't wiped out, and then the storm came back again. For you, and I fear that it is coming back again. Like it did in 1815."

"That's not possible," Gary said.

"You and I are not possible, Gary. Mother Nature fucked up, and she knows it."

"But she, the storm did not come back after you switched places, realities. Nothing happened, so why would the storm come back now and wipe everything, everyone out?" Gary jumped to his feet. "Me being here shouldn't be a factor."

"Only one version of myself came through, Gary. You had two." Detective Green stood up from his chair. "There were two of you. First, it was the original Gary and then that crazed version of himself. Then, it was you and your killer half, who I don't regret killing. He killed a lot of women in this town, but like I said, there were two of you here in this reality. Two, so yes, that storm is coming back just like it did in 1815. And we are all in danger, Gary. You need to stop it."

"Me? I don't know if I can. I have no idea. It's a fucking storm," Gary said, now standing a short distance away from Detective Green. "This is fucking insane!"

"You have to try, or we are all dead." He walked toward the newspaper article and stared at it.

"So, what do we do?" Gary looked at the newspaper article. "What do I do?"

"Can't you feel it? The storm's coming back. It's close."

Gary realized that he could feel the storm and cringed. "Holly," Gary said. "No, I can't let her die. Not again. I can't, so I don't have a choice."

"Neither did I," Detective Green said. "So, we wait. No matter how long it takes, we wait until the storm is finally here, and then you do whatever you need to. But you end this."

"I will," Gary said. "Why six months? Why that time frame?"

"I wish I knew," Detective Green said. "But I don't, and it's just about time now. You'll know when the storm calls for you."

Gary remained at the detective's house. As the days passed by and he recovered from his attack, he could feel the storm. It was an odd sensation like the air was electrified, and it was getting closer. And it wanted him, but what did he ever do to deserve this? Now, the clouds were rolling in, and behind it was the storm. And Gary knew it was time, but where was Detective Green? He couldn't wait for him. The storm was just about here, and this needed to end. But would he still be here afterward?

Lightning flashed in the distance. Thunder fired its warning shots. The storm was here, but the detective wasn't. Gary couldn't wait anymore, but before he confronts the storm, he had to say good-bye to Holly.

Getting a cab in this neighborhood proved to be a little difficult, but as he moved past residential roads to the main ones, he finally found a cab that he could hail. He gave the driver Holly's address and then turned around to stare at the sky. Traffic lights swung above the cab as it made its way toward Holly's home, and the skies opened up. Gary prayed to see Holly one last time.

An answer to his prayers was her house coming into view. He gave the cab driver a twenty and bolted from the car. The storm was fierce as it tried to pull him back, but he managed to move to the back of the house again. And again, the glass slider door was left unlocked. Gary found Holly sleeping on the couch.

Brown eyes flashed open. A body sat upright. Lightning lit up the room, danced off the coffee table, and flashed across her fear and grief. The grandfather clock ticked to her heartbeat, and a crash of thunder followed. Trying to press out the storm, she covered her ears, but it was too late. Gary was gone.

A shadow moved against the wall. She pulled the covers closer to her and tried to see through the darkness, but every time the lightning flashed, the shadow swiftly moved away. Someone was there. Someone was watching her. Was it him? "Gary," she whispered.

"Yes," he whispered back.

"Gary." Excitement filled her voice, but why was he hiding from her? "Where have you been? It's been six months."

"I'm sorry, Holly." He crept toward the wall and pushed himself into it. "Go to sleep. It'll be okay."

"Go to sleep?" Despite the storm raging outside, Holly realized that she was still really tired and found it hard to move off the couch. "Please, Gary. Don't leave me. Please, don't leave like that again. I thought… I thought you were gone for good." She fell back into a deep sleep.

"If only you knew," he whispered.

Gary touched her face, but she didn't wake up. He leaned over, and his lips brushed against hers. He kissed her and half expected her to wake up screaming like before. But she didn't, and she smiled. "I love you, Holly," he said. "Most of us loved you. Good-bye."

Gary walked outside. The storm was waiting. Rain pounded the pavement. Lightning flashed in front of him, and the thunder screamed. All her fury for him, but she was the one that screwed up. "You want me? Here I am, you bitch!" He stepped into the driveway. "Come and get me, but do not destroy this town. Do not kill her! Take me instead! Come on! Hit me!" Lightning struck the ground.

## CHAPTER SEVEN

"I'm sorry." Detective Green looked up from his desk. "The case has gone cold, Holly."

"Meaning?" She wavered before him as Bill stared down at his feet. "What?"

"There are no leads to follow," Detective Green said.

"So, that's it?" She looked from the detective to Bill. "We give up?"

"I'm sorry." Pushing fifty, Detective Green was feeling his age, and he was tired. Hoping to find the lawyer, he had chased every lead, but most of the leads were dead ends. As time went on, the leads ran out, and the case became cold. He wanted to tell Holly to move on, to declare her husband dead, but every time he looked into her eyes, he saw hope. She wasn't giving up, but maybe, it was time that she did. "Holly, it's time. Time to consider that Gary is…"

"Alive. I saw him last night."

"What?"

"Holly." Bill shook his head at her. "It was a dream."

"No, Bill. It wasn't. He was in the house, and I spoke to him." Detective Green pulled out a pad and pen from his desk. "He was there, and then I went back to sleep." The detective took the pad and pen and placed it back into his desk. "He was there. Gary was there."

"Did you see him," Detective Green asked.

"Yeah. I mean… It was dark, but he was there."

"Holly?" Detective Green leaned back in his seat. "Did you see him?"

"No." Holly looked from Detective Green to Bill. "He was hiding from me."

"Why would he do that?"

"I don't know. You're the damn detective." Holly immediately regretted the anger in her voice, but the sympathetic look on the detective's face made her angrier. "You know what? Forget it. Just forget it. I didn't see him. Happy?" She glared at Bill. "I'm out of here."

Bill waited until Holly was further away from them. "And the Oscar goes to…" He pointed at Detective Green, who smiled at him. Bill smiled back. "It would be easier if we could just tell her."

"No. Let him do that," Detective Green said.

"I thought he was gone. Is he gone?" Bill watched Detective Green shrug. "So, this might not be over with?"

"It's over. The storm's not coming back." He watched Bill sigh. "For now." He ignored the look on Bill's face and watched Holly talk to his son. "Bill, thank you for helping me before at Holly's house."

"It was Gary, but it wasn't. I just wish that I got a chance to say goodbye to my friend." Bill looked over at Holly and Eric. "What are you going to do about your son?"

"Let him be. He might be like a dog with a bone sometimes, but somehow, someway, he'll figure it out on his own."

"And if he tells her?"

"Gary did love her. I think most of them did. Do me a favor? Chase my son away, so I can have a smoke outside."

"Gladly." They both laughed. "Dinner at Earl's? Tomorrow night?"

"Tomorrow night at Earl's, but the first round's on me." He chuckled as Bill interrupted Eric and Holly's conversation. His son looked at him, but he merely shrugged. He waited a beat for his son to leave, but of course not until after his son gave him his lunch, which he tossed onto his desk. Then, he grabbed his smokes and lighter out of a desk drawer.

"Hey, I thought you quit," Harold said.

"Hell no."

"But you did."

Detective Green looked at Harold. "How's that serial killer case going?"

"It's the darndest thing. It stopped. The killings just stopped." Harold looked over at a guy sitting handcuffed in a chair nearby. "That guy over there? Marc. He's definitely a rapist and killer, but he's not the serial killer. That person just seems to have vanished into thin air."

Detective Green laughed, and his partner stared at him. "Damn shame," he said. "I would've liked to have killed him myself." He walked outside and stuck a cigarette between his lips.

"Nasty habit. You should quit."

"Mind your business." He turned around and saw Gary and the scar on his face. "You're still here?"

"She didn't take me. I don't know why." Gary remained standing behind Detective Green.

"I see." Detective Green lit his cigarette. "That night when I saved your life and killed the other one, I brought him outside. As soon as I did, lightning struck him." He blew smoke away from Gary. "Maybe, she didn't take you because one of you has to remain in this reality."

"I think you're right. Did you give Holly the letter that I left at your house?"

"No. Not yet." The detective reached into his pocket and withdrew a white envelope with Holly's name on it. "She's not giving up on you, especially after last night."

"I had to say good-bye. Just in case, you didn't give her the letter." He took the envelope from the detective.

"I would've given it to her. Eventually." Detective Green smoked his cigarette. "So, now what?"

"I don't know."

Detective Green dropped his cigarette to the ground and stepped on it. "You got a second chance, Gary. Now, you have to ask yourself something."

"What?"

"What kind of life do you want to live here?" He pointed at Gary's scar. "That kind of life or a better one? And don't make Holly wait too long for you to come back."

"I won't. Thank you, Detective Green."

"Brian." He held out his hand, and Gary shook it. "See you around." He stepped away.

"Hey, that novel you're writing. What's it called?"

"Waken," Detective Green replied and walked inside the building.

Gary took a cab around the Town of Waken. He passed by the law office. Then, Earl's. Finally, Holly's house. He sat outside for a while next to his rental, which was still parked where he left it. He didn't see Holly's mother's car, so he knew the coast was clear. Slowly, he made his way around back and into the house. They really need to lock this door, he thought as he sat on the couch, but he knew that he could not stay there. He walked into the kitchen and picked up the phone, dialing the law office number.

"Good morning, Javin and Henders Associates." Gary froze. "Hello?" He opened his mouth to talk, but only his breathing was heard. "Hello? Can I help you?" He hung up the phone.

"Damn it, Gary," he cursed at himself. "Don't do this again." He took a breath, waited a few minutes, and then dialed the number again.

"Good morning... Good afternoon, Javin and Henders Associates."

"Good afternoon." No answer. "Hello?"

"Hello."

"So good to hear your voice." He smacked himself on the forehead.

"Who... Who is this? Can I help you?"

"That was some bad storm. Never seen anything like it."

"It was just a thunderstorm last night. Nothing else."
"Not like six months ago." A long pause. "I have to ask."
"What?"
"Why were you in the hospital afterward?"
"Holly." He heard Bill's voice, and he sounded angry. "Who's that on the phone?" There was a brief tug of war before Bill's voice boomed through the phone. "Hello? Hello? Who is this?"
"It's me," Gary said. "Good-bye, Bill." He hung up the phone.

Gary moved up the stairs and headed for Holly's room. For whatever reason, he stopped at the guest room and opened the door. To his surprise, he saw a baby's crib filled with stuffed animals. He took a step closer and noticed a soft, pink blanket in the crib. "I have a daughter. That's why she was in the hospital." He cried. "I have a baby girl."

Detective Green's words echoed inside his head, "What kind of life do you want to live here?"

"A good one," Gary said. "For Holly and our child."

Gary left the room and entered Holly's bedroom. He opened the window and looked outside. The skies were clear, and he smiled. He moved over to the closet and grabbed some more of his clothes. Well, the other Gary's clothes. He also went through the dresser drawers. He didn't want to give the impression that he had packed up and run, but he wanted Holly to know that he was still alive. Then, he noticed their wedding picture on the dresser. Well, the other Gary's wedding picture. He gently lifted it up, sat on the bed, and stared at it. They were happy. They were in love. "We'll be like that again." He left the picture on the bed and placed the envelope on top of it. "This isn't good-bye, Holly," he said. "Just good-bye for now. We'll see each other again."

He returned to the guestroom, picked up the soft, pink blanket and wrapped his pocket watch in it. He gently placed the blanket and pocket watch back into the crib. He touched a stuffed, blue elephant nearby. He smiled and left the room.

# OTHER PUBLICATIONS BY MELISSA R. MENDELSON

*Better Off Here*
"A Collection of Dystopian Short Stories"
2019

    Link to buy: https://www.amazon.com/Better-Off-Here-Melissa-Mendelson/dp/1796753297/

*Stories Written Along COVID Walls*
"A Collection of Short Stories involving COVID"
2020

    Link to buy: https://www.amazon.com/Stories-Written-Along-COVID-Walls/dp/B08GB1MKFK

*This Will Remain With Us*
    "Poetry Collection involving being a Frontline Worker during COVID"
    Wild Ink Publishing, 2022

    Link to buy: https://www.amazon.com/This-Will-Remain-Melissa-Mendelson/dp/1958531103/

*Waken*
"A surreal novella, contemporary fiction"
Available on Amazon in eBook and paperback.
2023

    Link to buy: https://www.amazon.com/Waken-Dream-Melissa-Mendelson-ebook/dp/B00Q9KBWLQ/

## ABOUT THE AUTHOR

Melissa R. Mendelson is a Poet and Horror, Science-Fiction and Dystopian Short Story Author. Her stories have been published by Sirens Call Publications, Dark Helix Press, Altered Reality Magazine, Transmundane Press, Owl Canyon Press, Wild Ink Publishing, and The Yard: Crime Blog.